Good Time Boyfriend

A FIRST TIME SERIES NOVEL

By
Carrie Ann Ryan

GOOD TIME BOYFRIEND
A Wilder Brothers Novel
By: Carrie Ann Ryan
© 2023 Carrie Ann Ryan

Cover Art by Sweet N Spicy Designs
Photo by Wander Aguiar Photography

Good Time Boyfriend

Special Edition

The First Time Series

Carrie Ann Ryan

Praise for Carrie Ann Ryan

"Count on Carrie Ann Ryan for emotional, sexy, character driven stories that capture your heart!" – Carly Phillips, NY Times bestselling author

"Carrie Ann Ryan's romances are my newest addiction! The emotion in her books captures me from the very beginning. The hope and healing hold me close until the end. These love stories will simply sweep you away." ~ NYT Bestselling Author Deveny Perry

"Carrie Ann Ryan writes the perfect balance of sweet and heat ensuring every story feeds the soul." - Audrey Carlan, #1 New York Times Bestselling Author

"Carrie Ann Ryan never fails to draw readers in with passion, raw sensuality, and characters that pop off the page. Any book by Carrie Ann is an absolute treat." – New York Times Bestselling Author J. Kenner

"Carrie Ann Ryan knows how to pull your heartstrings and make your pulse pound! Her wonderful Redwood Pack series will draw you in and keep you reading long into the night. I can't wait to see what comes next with the new generation, the Talons. Keep them coming, Carrie Ann!" –Lara Adrian, New York Times bestselling author of CRAVE THE NIGHT

"With snarky humor, sizzling love scenes, and brilliant, imaginative worldbuilding, The Dante's Circle series reads as if Carrie Ann Ryan peeked at my personal wish list!" – NYT Bestselling Author, Larissa Ione

"Carrie Ann Ryan writes sexy shifters in a world full of passionate happily-ever-afters." – *New York Times* Bestselling Author Vivian Arend

"Carrie Ann's books are sexy with characters you can't help but love from page one. They are heat and heart blended to perfection." *New York Times* Bestselling Author Jayne Rylon

Carrie Ann Ryan's books are wickedly funny and deliciously hot, with plenty of twists to keep you guessing. They'll keep you up all night!" USA Today Bestselling Author Cari Quinn

"Once again, Carrie Ann Ryan knocks the Dante's Circle series out of the park. The queen of hot, sexy, enthralling paranormal romance, Carrie Ann is an author not to miss!" *New York Times* bestselling Author Marie Harte

GOOD TIME BOYFRIEND

A new town. A new bar. A new life.

At least, that's what I'm hoping for.

I moved to Denver to try to piece my family back together, but I have no idea how to do that.

Then the most beautiful woman I've ever seen walks into my bar, and I think things are looking up.

She needs a fake boyfriend for the night and I'm all too eager to play along.

But when the sun rises, reality settles in and I know I want more. Only I don't think she's ready for what I have to give.

I want to be more than a good time, but I know what I'm good for. I need control. And she's far too innocent.

Only when something happens that changes the rules,

we'll have to make a choice quickly, or we could lose everything before it even starts.

To Brandi,

I promise to rest and play. This story showed me how.

Chapter One

Heath

There was nothing like the view of the Rockies in Denver, Colorado. Okay, there was nothing like the view of the Rockies anywhere. I used to live in Portland, Oregon, so I knew trees and mountains and stunning. However, seeing the mountains and trees in Portland without a cloudy or rainy sky didn't happen often. Oregon was beautiful, but Colorado? It called to me. Maybe it was just the novelty of it, since I had only lived here a year, but I didn't think so.

This was home now, despite everything that happened when I had first moved here.

I hadn't moved here for the mountains. Hadn't moved here for the sunny days, high altitude, dry heat, or blizzards. I'd moved here for family. A family that I was determined to bring together in a way we hadn't ever been before.

Of course, that meant I needed a damn job.

"Are you done drooling over the mountains yet? We need to get inside and open up."

"I just can't believe they're real. They don't fucking look real."

Ace sighed at my side, but stuffed his hands in his pockets, and looked out at the majestic beauty of the Rockies with me.

I hadn't realized I would love Denver like this. That it would call to me. And it really did look like someone had painted those peaks and valleys in front of me.

"I still think they look better right after a storm. When the clouds begin to part and they look almost purple."

I turned to Ace and grinned. "Yeah, you're right. I've been here a year now and I've seen every season."

Ace rolled his eyes before he reached out and squeezed my shoulder. "It's Denver. You've only seen six of the twenty thousand seasons we have. And sometimes six in one day."

I snorted, but I agreed with him. You could wake up with snow in the morning and end up wearing a tank top by the evening. I was getting used to it—at least I thought so.

"Come on, let's go open the bar."

I smiled as I turned towards the building behind us.

We were right on the outskirts of downtown Denver. Still in the hustle and bustle and close enough for foot traffic, but also near enough to the train station that there was room to breathe, and you could see the mountains from all sides. I loved knowing where west was, because that was the direction of downtown's skyline.

"You ready for today? We have a long one."

I nodded as we stepped into Lost and Found. Before I even decided to move here, Ace had asked if I wanted to join him in a new endeavor. I had owned a bar in Portland, one that had been doing really damn well. I had been the sole owner of the place, and finding and managing staff that could actually keep up had taken a toll.

When Ace asked if I had wanted a change, I leaped on the opportunity. Not just because it was Ace, a man I had known for years, but because Greer was here.

Lost and Found had been Ace's idea, and I had bought in.

We had lost something growing up, and we needed to find it. That wasn't like me. I wasn't sentimental. I was the guy who got shit done because I knew my parents weren't going to do it. I had done my best to keep my brothers safe. Both Luca and August had gone through hell, and I hadn't been able to keep the worst from them, and our parents hadn't even tried.

We hadn't even been allowed to get to know our baby sister because of our parents.

But that's what happens when your parents got married and divorced multiple times. Their first divorce was when I was a child, not even ten years old, my siblings were even younger. Of course, August was my twin, but I was the eldest, and I took that role seriously. Luca had been an infant, a baby just learning to walk. Greer was a couple years younger than August and me.

After that divorce, our dad took the boys, and our mom took Greer. Because apparently they had seen both versions of *The Parent Trap* and thought that was a wonderful fucking idea.

That made me roll my eyes to this day but, unlike the movie, there was no happy ever after. Even though our parents got back together, and we had a few years with our sister, trying to get to know her again, I never got to know her as well as I wanted. I was never there to protect her when things got bad, and when our parents got divorced again, they split us up again, like our opinions didn't matter. We had gone to different schools, and while I had my brothers and they had me, Greer had no one.

When our parents got together for the third time, we had all given up. We were adults, and they couldn't split us up if they divorced again. Except we had split ourselves up. Greer moved out here to be with her best friend who was originally from the Denver area. They opened a shop of their own, a little coffee and bakery place near a tattoo shop, that kicked ass.

It was time to be with my little sister. Only, it wasn't going as well as I'd hoped, and it felt like it was my fault. But I didn't want to think about that.

"You're all in your head. Are you okay?"

I turned to Ace and nodded. "I'm fine. Sorry. Let me go start setting up."

"You do that. Grace's working in the office today, doing paperwork so I don't have to. I'm so glad I'm marrying an accountant."

I smiled, shaking my head. "I don't know what we would do without her. Yeah, we would probably figure it out, but Grace actually knowing what she's doing without having to ask a thousand questions? Yes, you're marrying the right woman."

"Did I just hear that you're marrying me for my math skills?" Grace asked as she came in.

While Ace was well above six foot, big and bearded and full of tattoos, Grace was a tiny slip of a woman. She had bright red hair, luscious curves, and could probably fit in my pocket. She also had the biggest laugh and smile, and her face lit up every time she saw Ace. But the best part? My growly and grumpy friend lit up right back.

"I think he is also marrying you for your spreadsheets."

She grinned at me and then went to her tippy toes to

kiss the bottom of Ace's beard. He leaned down for her, and they kissed a bit more. I cleared my throat after a moment.

"I would ask if you'd like a room, but we share that office. I don't want to know what goes on when the door is closed."

Grace blushed, but Ace grinned. "Then we won't tell you."

I groaned. "Really? At least bleach it afterwards."

"And on that note, I'm going to go work on those spreadsheets. Alone. Because I don't trust you." She waved her finger at him.

Ace rolled his eyes. "Fine. I see how it is."

"You better." She waved us off. I laughed before going back to setting up.

We were open from three until one. I wouldn't be closing, our team would. Usually Ace and I didn't open together, but on days when Grace was here doing the accounting, we both wanted to be here in case there were any questions. And, frankly, even though I was still in my twenties, I liked being home to sleep in my own bed before midnight.

I set to work on the kegs and ensuring that all the glassware and prep were ready from the night before. I had oranges and lemons and limes to cut, more cherries to procure, and countless other things. Keeping the cherries in stock when everyone kept stealing them was a hazard of the business and meant that I had to hide them from my own staff. It was that way when I was a server and busboy when I was sixteen, and the problem had only gotten worse as time moved on.

The door opened before we were open for business and I looked up to see Greer walk in, making me smile.

My sister looked like us. Brown hair with subtle high-lights from the sun, bright light eyes, but in a petite frame.

While Luca was slightly smaller than August and me, he was still bigger than Greer by far. And Luca was bulking up from his day job, lifting huge sixty-to-eighty-pound dogs onto a vet table.

"Hey there, little sister. I didn't know you were coming in today." I moved around the bar so I could come up to her, arms outstretched. She smiled at me before wrapping her arms around my waist, hugging me tightly.

We stood there for a moment, taking it in, the situation still new enough that I wasn't quite sure when the novelty of it would wear off. We had been apart for so many years, and I hadn't known when she was sick or feeling grumpy or what her favorite book was. I hadn't known anything until we were old enough to be able to contact each other outside of our parents. They hadn't liked us calling the other house, connecting with the parent who hadn't chosen us.

I was getting to know this Greer, but I sure as hell missed the young Greer I never got to know.

Carrie Ann Ryan

We split apart, and she grinned at me. "I was in the area and figured I'd say hi."

"You work like twenty minutes west of here, and I thought you were closing today."

She nodded but held out her phone. "I had to meet with our backer, and since her shop is only a few blocks from here, I figured I'd walk to you to say hi before I caught the light rail back."

"Do you want my car? You're welcome to drive it back."

She waved me off. I knew I sounded a bit eager. I just wanted to protect her, to help her. The fact that Greer was now engaged to not one, but two men meant that I didn't need to protect her. She had the two loves of her life for that. Hell, she could protect herself. The fact that Greer's men also happened to run a security business? Well, that meant I felt a little out of sorts. A little unneeded. But that was on me. Never on her.

"My car is at my place. But with traffic because of an accident on 25, I decided to take public transportation. It's really okay. I have a pass and everything."

"And I realize it's better for the environment, but I just like to give you things."

"I know. And I'm grateful. And I did bring something for you." She handed over the paper bag and I could smell the deliciousness before I even opened it.

8

Plump pastries, bagels, and other goodies—at least a dozen.

My mouth watered, and she smiled at me. "I know you have drinks here, but I figured pastries from not only our shop, but Haley's too would be welcome."

"Did I hear the word pastry?" Ace asked, practically pushing me out of the way. "There's my Greer." Ace hugged her tightly as Greer laughed, and Grace came running in, throwing her arms around both of them.

It was so easy for them, becoming family without over-thinking it. It felt like I was trying to do so much for her, and failing, because she didn't need me. But I was still so damn glad I moved here. I would be missing this. I would be missing the chance to be the overprotective asshole brother.

I just needed to figure out what else I needed to be.

"Anyway, I have to head back. Enjoy the pastries. I'll see you guys for dinner this weekend?" she asked, and both Ace and Grace nodded.

"Yeah, if not before."

"I love the fact that you live close enough to me that you can come into the coffee shop every morning if you want. I would say it's like old times, but we both know it's not." She rolled her eyes and I felt the kick to the gut, even though she didn't. She had found her steadiness, her foundation. And while I knew she still carried the same pain that we all did, she was moving forward. I thought my

Carrie Ann Ryan

brothers were doing the same. I was the one who needed to get in line.

"Then we just have to make up for it," I said quickly, and she nodded. We hugged and she headed out. Ace went back to setting up, Grace back to the office, and I swallowed hard and did what I did best—I worked.

The early shift was nice, because you got tourists and some regulars, and nobody was loud and obnoxious yet. That always made me happy.

By the time seven o'clock rolled around however, the din started to grow, the noise unending. I didn't mind it though, I wouldn't have opened a bar if I hated it. I liked getting to know people, to hear their problems and act as if I knew what I was doing.

I didn't always, but I could pretend.

"Hey, whatever happened with that woman?" Ace asked as I worked on a martini, straight-up, extra cold, with a twist.

I frowned before I remembered, I knew exactly what he was talking about. "I don't even know her name. She was just here on our opening night, and she was gorgeous. Not quite sure why you brought her up?"

"Because you have talked to at least twenty gorgeous women tonight, all of them hitting on you, and you haven't done a thing about it."

"You know I don't hit back. This is a job. Not a stomping ground."

"So you say."

"You met Grace in a grocery store, both of you trying to find an organic cereal from your list, and you reached it for her because she couldn't. That's a meet-cute. At a bar? Not so much."

"Look at you, knowing the phrase 'meet-cute.'"

"Greer has me reading romance novels. I like them. Didn't think I would, but I do."

The guy at the bar snickered but I ignored him. He wasn't going to tip me anyway. He had been in before and he never did.

"True, but I was just thinking about the last time your heart did that little pitter-patter thing."

"Pitter-patter? Maybe you need to be reading those novels."

"Grace would probably like it. I could learn a thing or two."

"Or seven," the woman at the end of the bar said as she sipped her old-fashioned, before waving and turning to talk to her girlfriend.

"Okay, so I know what I'm reading next. Or should I ask Greer?"

"Take a look at my ereader later. You'll see what you need."

"That's good. Now I have to get back to the bachelorette party. Pray for me."

I rolled my eyes as I handed over my next drink and got back to work.

"Hey, are you Heath?" a deep voice asked.

The bar began to quiet down a bit and I frowned before I looked at the group of people on the other side of the bar.

They all had dark hair, dark eyes, and fair white skin. And if they hadn't been cut from the same cloth, I wasn't a very good bartender. So, they had to be siblings. And the way they were frowning at me had me a little worried.

I had never seen these people before. I might not be the best at names, but I was damn good at faces.

"I am. Is there something I can do for you guys?"

"Yeah," one of the men said. All three women and two men were glaring at me, arms folded over their chest. Hell, this wasn't going to go well. "You can tell us why you dumped our baby sister," the man continued.

The bar got quiet, and I just stood there wondering who the hell these people were.

They had called me by name, so they weren't confusing me with my twin, unless August had used my name in a relationship? No, we had never done that, had always found it skeevy. What was going on?

"You broke our baby sister's heart. After a year of being together. You just dump her and walk away and say no hard feelings? And you wouldn't even meet us throughout your whole relationship. What are you hiding?" one of the women asked.

Before I could say anything, and before Ace could rush over and help out, another woman ran in, eyes wide, hair fluttering behind her.

I blinked because I knew this face. *I knew her.*

Long, wavy blond hair, high cheekbones, plump lips, and a body a man would die for. This was the woman that my heart went pitter-patter for. *And I didn't even know her fucking name.*

It was as if Ace had conjured her.

She ran in, arms outstretched, and stood between me and the five people who were staring me down.

"I'm so sorry. This is all a mistake," she pleaded to me before she whirled on them. "Why the hell are you guys here?"

These were her siblings? I didn't even know her name and, apparently, I had dumped her.

"He hurt you. Did you think we were just going to walk away? You're our baby sister."

She looked nothing like the others, but then again, most siblings didn't look like replicas like mine.

"And that gives you the right to come into his place of business and badger him? You're embarrassing me."

She hadn't denied it though. Hadn't denied we had been in a relationship that I didn't remember.

"Um, excuse me?" I began, but one of the siblings just waved me off.

Well, that was going to get annoying soon.

"He hurt you. Of course, we're going to protect you, Devney."

Devney. Her name was Devney.

She looked over her shoulder at me, and the pain in her eyes hit me like a punch to the chest. Well hell. I now knew her name, and I knew she had to be in some predicament that she was going to explain to me later. But for now, I could at least help her get rid of that pain in her eyes.

I leaned forward and sighed. "I'm so sorry, Devney. So damn sorry."

She blinked at me, confusion in her gaze, then all hell broke loose behind her.

Chapter Two

Devney

This couldn't be happening. It had to be a dream. No, a nightmare. Because the man that I had made up, based on a real encounter with a real person, was now standing on the other side of the bar, looking at my five stepsiblings as if they had lost their damn minds. And in reality, they had.

I could not believe the five of them had decided to show up unannounced and stand up for me—all for a lie.

Guilt warred with mortification, and I wasn't sure what was going to win.

I didn't have time to think much about it, because now we were not only making a scene, but it was going to get worse.

Especially with the way that my eldest stepbrother was glaring.

Andy had a temper. It had cooled somewhat when he married Kendra, but it was a temper. Of course, Maureen's icy temper was usually the one I had to worry about. Elizabeth, Paige, and Lee were sometimes more reasonable.

Except for the fact that I was their baby sister, maybe not by blood, but no matter what, they would always take care of me, even if that meant being overbearing, radical, and never leaving me alone.

They were the reason I had to tell a tiny white lie, one that had steamrolled itself into a full-blown fantasy. I had nearly sent myself flowers to make the fake relationship look real, and only stopped myself when I realized the delusion had gotten a little scary.

A tiny little lie that was now going to not only embarrass me, but possibly hurt a man I didn't even know. I only knew his name because of the one time I'd met him at the opening of this very bar.

And here he stood, gaze locked on my five stepsiblings, and I stood between them, hands outstretched, trying to keep them safe. I felt like I was in that dinosaur movie where Chris Pratt was trying to keep the velociraptors away by holding out his hands, but I knew that one minute, if I wasn't careful, these dinosaurs would bite. I didn't know if it would be Heath, or my five siblings who snapped their jaws first. I was just grateful that my younger half-siblings, all five of them, weren't old enough to actually be in a bar.

Yes, I had ten siblings. Five of them I gained by marriage, the other five were born after my mother married my stepfather.

It was weird, being the middle child of two distinct and yet connected families. Yet here I was, standing between the steps and Heath, like I always did between the house and the steps.

Not that we used labels when it came to family. We were all siblings, all brothers and sisters.

It was just easier when I was categorizing them to add the titles. I still had no idea how my mother dealt with eleven children.

I could barely keep up with one tiny lie that was no longer tiny.

I turned to Heath, my eyes a little wide, and I was really hoping that he couldn't see the panic there.

"Excuse me?" Heath asked. I didn't really have answers for this. Other than burying my soul and saying that I was a complete liar and a chicken shit when it came to trying to get out of my siblings' shadows.

I just hadn't wanted to be set up on dates. I didn't want them to worry about "little old me" and the fact that I didn't have anybody.

Lee cleared his throat. "He hurt you. Of course, we're going to protect you, Devney."

I held back a wince as I looked at Heath over my shoulder. I didn't know how to fix this. There was no way I *could* fix this. Other than telling the truth, and dealing with the consequences. That was the best option.

I opened my mouth and knew that if I told the truth right now, it would be over quicker. And then I could go home and hide under my blankets and never leave again.

But then Heath leaned forward and sighed. He put his arms on the bar top and looked at me with such genuine concern, I was truly afraid that I had entered an alternate dimension where there was no right or wrong or up and down. Just insanity.

"I'm so sorry, Devney. So damn sorry."

I blinked at him, confusion etching my features, as my siblings all began talking at once. They spoke over each other as usual, and while I could understand them because I lived with them long enough that I knew all their ins and outs, I had a feeling that Heath had no idea what these five were saying. But then again, I wasn't really listening to them. It was an echo chamber where they were talking to one another, and I just stared at Heath. Had he just lied for me? This stranger?

How many women came up to him in bars with their family screaming behind them wondering why he had broken up with them?

Or was this an alternate dimension where I actually had dated him?

"Devney and I are just on a break. We wanted to make sure we figured out how to be friends first. You know how it is." He was saying things. His voice was so rough and sexy, and yet it didn't actually feel real.

No, it couldn't be real.

But with those bright blue eyes and dark hair, he made it hard for me to think of anything else.

His hair was longer on top and brushed back and cut short on the sides. He had a big beard that went well past his chin, but it was structured, as if he actually cared for it. And that just made me think of what else he could care for.

I held back a groan, wondering what was wrong with me. Just because he had been my imaginary boyfriend for so long, didn't mean I was allowed to ogle him like this.

Right?

"What?" Andy asked, his gaze narrowing.

I held my hands up between them once again. "This is really none of y'all's business."

"You're our baby sister. Of course, it's our business," Maureen said.

She was the eldest of us all and had that big-sister energy. She always took care of us. Even if I didn't want to be taken care of.

I just wanted to hide and forget my lie. But for some reason he seemed to be going along with it.

What the hell?

"So, you're saying you guys are just on a break. Like that TV show? Because it didn't really work out in the end for them." Elizabeth narrowed her gaze.

"They were on a break though," Paige put in.

"But he still cheated. Because you don't go out and sleep with the first person you see right after you take a break," Andy interrupted.

"Is that what you did?" Lee asked, and I huffed out a breath.

"We can go through the merits of a show that's been over for twenty years anytime you want, except for right now. This really isn't any of your business and you're embarrassing me. Just go home, okay?"

"We are making a scene," Elizabeth said as she looked around.

"Please go," I said, mortification setting in as I realized people were indeed looking at us.

"So, you really want us to just leave you with your ex?"

"I'm not going to hurt her," Heath put in.

Andy snorted. "You already did."

There had to be a hole I could jump in and bury myself. I mean, any moment now a cavern would open up and just take me to my isolation. That would be wonderful.

Sadly though, it didn't happen. Heath gave me a look

that said that I owed him. I didn't know why he was playing along. Maybe this was part of the bartender's repertoire. But I was going to go with it. Or find a hole to bury myself in.

"Seriously. I'm an adult. You need to go, this is his place of business. Please stop. Go home to all of your spouses and kids. You do not need to be here. Please."

"This isn't over," Lee said as he pointed at Heath, before Elizabeth sighed and pulled them back. Elizabeth was always the calmer one.

It still felt like I was the baby sister that had been brought in at a weird time. It hadn't helped that the next five had been born so quickly after my mother had married their father.

And they were just as feral about protecting the babies as they were about protecting me. Then again, I was the same way. If anyone hurt any of my ten siblings, I would fight to the death.

But for some reason, both sets seemed to want to protect me.

Maybe it was because I was the only one with my name in the family. The only one not a full-blood relation to others.

So they wanted to protect me.

And I had lied because of it.

They finally left and people started going back about

their business. I was grateful I wasn't the center of attention anymore. Except that I was the sole focus of somebody's attention.

I cleared my throat and turned to look at Heath.

I was ready to be kicked out of the bar, with a lifetime ban.

How many times had something like this happened to him? Probably more than I cared to count. Or maybe this was brand new, and this wasn't something that he did on a regular basis. You know, placate the crazy person and their crazier family.

I had never even had a boyfriend before, other than the fake one. It wasn't that I didn't want one, it just hadn't come up. I'd been a little busy. And a little shy. And here I was, standing alone in a bar, knowing that if I wasn't careful, my family could show up again and drag me out.

This wasn't embarrassing at all.

"So, Devney, is it?"

I winced. "I am so sorry."

"You want a drink?" he asked, nodding towards the bar. "On the house."

"Oh, I'd love a drink, and I'll pay. Because, well, I think you've done a lot already."

"Oh, I think we're both going to need a drink after this."

"Can I get a lemon drop?"

"Do you like sugar on the lemon?"

"Not really. I'm sorry."

"Don't apologize. At least not for ordering the drink how you like it. And I don't think you need to apologize for what just happened. But I would love to know exactly what the fuck just happened."

"And I would love to know why you went along with it," I said as I sat at the end of the bar. He turned toward the other bearded man and said something too quiet for me to hear, but neither of them looked in my direction. Maybe they weren't talking about me and how insane I was. But I wouldn't be surprised if they were. After all, nearly half of my family had just shown up to lambaste him over something he hadn't done.

I really needed to leave. Why was I staying at the scene of the crime?

"So," he said, as he handed a chilled glass to me, filled to the brim with a delicious looking cocktail. "Take a sip, and then you can introduce yourself to me for real this time."

I sighed, and then took a sip. It was sweet and tart all at the same time, and was so good I held back a groan. Or at least I tried to.

When it escaped my lips, Heath raised a brow, his eyes darkening.

"This is delicious."

"Good. I'm glad. Now, Devney, is it?"

Mortified, I set down my glass, and sighed. "Hi, I'm Devney Womack. We've met once before."

"I remember," he said, his voice a deep growl.

I froze, because it had just been that one time. Opening night, when I'd come in with my friend Addison before she went back to finish grad school. Addison had only had one year left and had been here for break. We'd come in to see the new place, I had met gazes with the bearded bartender, and had an instant crush. Of course, I hadn't spoken to him, hadn't seen him beyond those few moments, and then when we left, I'd put him out of my mind.

Or at least I'd tried.

"I saw you and read your little name tag," I said, gesturing towards his shirt.

He snorted. "Okay. I guess I was the first person to pop into your mind for your little... What was it, a daydream?"

I rolled my eyes. "It wasn't like I thought it was real. You see, I have five stepsiblings." I gestured towards the door where they'd left, and Heath's gaze widened for a moment. "Only five? They seem so much larger in the group."

"Tell me about it. I also have five half-siblings that are younger than me."

He set down the glass he had been drying. "You have

ten siblings?" he asked, his voice rising just enough that someone looked over.

I blushed and ducked my head. "Yes. And I try not to think about things like that. You know, about the fact that my mother and stepfather must really love each other," I said as he threw his head back and laughed.

He was gorgeous when he did. I asked myself again why hadn't I ever had a boyfriend? Yes, my siblings were overprotective. Yes, I had been focused on school and life and being shy, but if I could sit here and have a drink with the man who had been part of my lie, why couldn't I have done it for real?

Then again, it wasn't as if my fake fantasy relationship was real at all.

"So, you're the middle child of middle children. That's got to suck. Tell me about it."

"They're overprotective because they're a few years older than me. I was the baby when they showed up. And when I didn't want them setting me up with random people, or worried about me, I sort of...made you up."

"I was the first person you thought of. You couldn't have made up a fake person?"

I threw my hands in the air and sighed. "Of course not. Because that's not what my brain does. It makes things complicated. I tried to get them off my back about dating, because I focused on my career, my life. And the fact that I don't know if I actually like people enough to date them." I stopped. "Not that you aren't lovely."

Heath waved me off. "No, tell me more."

"Shush," I said with a laugh.

"I get it. Dating's hard. I'm a bartender, so I like people. I have to, in order to do it."

"Anyway, they constantly worry about me, and it got so annoying that they were pressuring me into wanting to have what they have."

"And what's that?" he asked, his voice soft.

It was odd, because he was still making drinks for others, there were still groups of people around us, speaking loudly, going about their nights. And yet it felt like it was just the two of us.

This delusional fantasy of mine was starting to get a little weird. Or, possibly, beyond weird.

"I made you up because I needed an excuse, and then I couldn't just say you dumped me after a week, so it just became a thing. And rolled into this whole relationship that was completely fake, and a huge lie, and I hate myself for it. I should be strong enough to stand up to my family, but I didn't want them to be disappointed in me for not wanting to be with the people they were setting me up with. So, I made up a fake you."

"And apparently I dumped you?" Heath asked.

I sighed and rubbed my hands over my face.

"There's a meme that says every girl has an ex-boyfriend who was never her boyfriend. And I have no idea where that came from, but that became my random existence. At least when it came to not wanting to go on dates with people that my siblings thought I would be good with. I always had you as an excuse in my back pocket. But when they wanted me to go to a wedding, and bring you with me, I couldn't just conjure you up."

"That would be a little tricky. So, I did dump you."

"I said that we had mutually decided to end the relationship."

"And your family didn't believe that?"

"Apparently not," I said and took another sip. "Apparently even my fake relationships need a huge embarrassing resolution." I paused. "Why did you lie for me?"

He shrugged as he met my gaze. "Because you looked like you needed help. And I don't mind. I have siblings, too, and it is nice that they stood up for you, even though that might have been a bit too much."

I sighed. "It doesn't help that I actually know your sister too," I said softly, more mortification setting in.

Heath's eyes widened. "You know Greer?"

"Yes. From her shop. So things got really sticky when I realized you were related to her, and new to town, and not just a figment of my imagination."

He just laughed and handed me a glass of water. "Well then, at least we both know that if you're friends with my sister, we're not weird stalker people. Just people that happen to lie to your family a bit. But at least they're letting you breathe. And you're having a drink. A delicious one."

One that was hitting me harder than I planned, because the next words out of my mouth were never meant to be uttered.

"So, not only am I a virgin, I'm a lying one. I hate lying."

I paused and looked up at him, his eyes deepening with a smokey color. Although why I thought I could actually read his emotions after just a few minutes, I didn't know.

But I honestly could not believe I just said that out loud.

"Well..." he cleared his throat, his voice rough.

"Please forget I said that. How about I pay you for this?"

"No, that's on the house. Did you drive?"

I shook my head. "No, I took the light rail."

"Good, because if you're blurting out things like that, maybe I made the drink too strong."

"I'm sorry. If you could just show me the nearest place I could jump off a cliff, that'd be wonderful."

He shook his head and gestured towards his friend. The two bearded men spoke softly, then Heath looked over at me. "Come on," he said.

"Where?"

"Let's go. I'm going to take you on a date. Make it real."

"What?"

"Well, I just gave you a very strong drink on I think an empty stomach."

At that moment my stomach rumbled and I blushed. "Maybe."

"So, let's get out of here. I'm not closing, and I'd like to get to know more about this fantasy relationship of ours."

"Please don't."

"Come on. And I can tell you all about the time I met this beautiful blonde and I couldn't stop thinking about her. But I never saw her again."

"Why would I want to hear about a blonde?"

He rolled his eyes and slid his hands through my hair.

"I wonder why."

"What?" I asked, trying to keep up with him. It was kind of hard to do that with that drink in my system.

"You know my sister. You know I'm a good guy. So, get to know the real one."

"Are you hitting on me right now?" I blurted.

"I'm trying. But then again, we've been dating for a while now, you should be used to my flirting."

I shook my head and chugged the rest of my water. "This is a weird dream."

"Maybe, but it's been an interesting one so far. Come on, let's go on a date. Make it real." Then he leaned forward. "And then we'll figure out exactly how far we're going to go into this lie."

I blushed when he took my hand. I wondered if it mattered if I never woke up from this dream.

Because I really didn't want to.

Chapter Three

Heath

This was probably a mistake, but it had been one hell of a night already. I might as well see where this mistake took us.

Because she was here.

The woman I hadn't stopped thinking about.

And she was a virgin.

Meaning I should probably stop thinking about her.

But I wouldn't.

At least not tonight.

But I wanted to know more.

That had always been a problem with me. Wanting to know more, and when I couldn't figure out the answers, frustration would settle in.

But there was just something about this evening,

something about the way she looked at me. As if she knew I didn't have the answers, but maybe I had something.

"Come on, there's a burger truck right at the edge of the parking lot. You're still in view of the bar, promise."

She looked at me dubiously, then out at the parking lot. "I still feel like this is how I get murdered."

I snorted, but she didn't really know me and had just left my bar with me. I couldn't downplay that.

"You know my sister. And you just proclaimed yourself to me. We just proclaimed ourselves to each other in front of your entire family. I feel like that bypasses a level of getting to know one another."

She sighed and ran her hand through her long blond hair. She was so gorgeous, so soft and goddess like. I was better than this normally at talking to women. Fuck, it was my job. And yet I felt like I was doing things wrong.

"That wasn't even half of my family."

I laughed, shaking my head. "I should be worried about that. But then again, my sister is marrying into a bigger family than yours."

She frowned. "I didn't know that was possible."

"Neither did I. We're a pretty small family." Though I didn't want to get into how small we were at times. Trying to explain that I had only lived with my sister for a few years of our childhood, and yet had always lived with my brothers confused people. Hell, it confused us, and we had lived it. Who the hell split up family like that, and prevented us from even talking with one another?

It was worse than a parent trap because we didn't want our parents back together. We just wanted our family together.

I just wanted my sister.

But I didn't need to think about that now. I had my family as together as it was going to be. I moved to this state with my brothers, we had packed up everything and started over here to be with our little sister. What more did we need?

"Okay, so this pity date of ours is walking across the parking lot and getting a hamburger. I don't mind that."

"I never said it was a pity date. It's just a way to ensure you're not lying."

"I hate lying. I don't know why I can't just stand up to them."

Although it was nearing the end of dinner time, there was still a decent line at the food truck. They did a good business, and we didn't mind them being here, because they made different burgers than we did. We fed business to each other, because they didn't have a liquor license, and we didn't do the gourmet specialty types of burgers with toppings I wouldn't even consider.

"I still can't believe that just happened," she said as we moved through the line.

"The fact that your family showed up at my bar? Or

the fact that you stayed?" I asked, not sure if I wanted the answer.

"How about both? I'm so sorry."

I shook my head. "Don't be. It was entertaining. I'd had a pretty boring day."

"I doubt that. You probably see so many different people throughout the day."

"True, but this was unique."

"I'm glad that I could entertain you with my idiocy."

I shook my head and gestured towards the menu on the side of the truck.

"You had your reasons. And, honestly, you showing up to protect me was quite nice."

"Yes, because you need my protection," she said with a dry laugh, before she narrowed her gaze at the menu. "Is there brie and some form of apricot jelly on that burger?"

"Yep. There's also one with an egg, and another with a salad, and sort of a pizza burger. I'm not quite sure how that one works."

"Is that one stuffed with mushrooms and cheese? Oh, my."

My mouth watered just thinking about it. I hadn't eaten anything since my early lunch, just after my sister left, and now I was starving. Normally I would just go home and either whip myself up something quick, or eat leftovers, if I wasn't closing. If that was the case, then I ate at the bar, and tried to drink some water when I got home, so that way I wasn't just falling right into bed, forgetting that I had a life. Not that I actually *had* a life, but I could pretend.

"How am I supposed to decide?"

She looked so earnest—and so damn sexy. This was going to be a problem. "We can each get a different one and share."

"You'd do that? Share with a stranger?"

"We aren't strangers. We've been dating for a year."

She shook her head, a small smile playing on her lips. "Now I really feel like I'm on a date with a murderer."

"Ouch. Calling your longtime boyfriend a murderer. That's not nice."

When she rolled her eyes, my smile widened. She was finally relaxing, and I couldn't help but be tempted. "I thought I was the insane one."

"Neither of us is insane. You needed to protect yourself, and you just happened to do it with a real person rather than a fake one."

"You were the first person I thought of." She paused. "Not in a stalker way. But because I had just seen you. You know. Sorry. I'm just going to shut up now."

I shook my head. "Come on, let's pick out what you want and I'll pick out something else that sounds good and we'll share. And I promise no big decisions need to be made. It's just a burger."

"Why do I feel like you're not quite telling the truth?"

I shrugged as we went up to the window. "I have no idea what you're talking about."

"Hey, Heath. Not closing tonight?" Jeff asked from the window.

"Nope, I opened. Ace should be done soon too, and our team is going to be closing tonight."

"Letting the baby birds out of the nest and leaving them in charge. Look at you. All business-owner like."

"You say that as if we're not going to be looking at the cameras we have stationed all around to make sure they're doing what they need to and don't need our help," I said dryly.

"True, that's why I work here way too many hours a day in my own truck, and I don't take days off." He turned to look at Devney, his eyes getting that smolder that said he found her attractive. I didn't mean to do it, knew I shouldn't, but I moved and put my arm near hers. I didn't wrap my arm around her, didn't stake my territory in a way that would be too obvious, but Jeff noticed.

He grinned and shook his head. "Oh, hello, I'm Jeff. Proprietor of this great establishment. What is your lovely name, and why are you with this lucky man?"

She rolled her eyes and looked between us. "I swear, all of you guys are so smooth." She cleared her throat. "I'm Devney. And I'm here because I'm starving, and we have a few things to talk about."

"Ooh, now I need to know what story is behind that.

But I don't pry. I don't have time to pry. Not with this line behind you."

I glared at the man before I leaned forward. "I'll take the mushroom and cheese stuffed burger with some ranch fries on the side."

"You've got it. What about you, babe?" Jeff didn't leer at her, which was the only reason I didn't punch my friend in the face. Though why I was this territorial, I didn't know.

"Oh good, that's sort of what I wanted, but that brie and jam one sounded amazing too."

"That's why your mouth started to water when you were looking at it."

"I didn't drool," she said as she dramatically wiped her mouth.

"Maybe just a little. Right here." I reached out and brushed my thumb along her cheek. Her eyes darkened and her mouth parted.

Jeff sighed. "Lucky bastard," he mumbled.

That brought both of us out of whatever the hell we were doing.

Devney cleared her throat. "Do you have a spicy fry? The ranch one sounds good, but I could use a kick."

I put my hand over my heart and staggered back. "Damn it, I knew you were perfect."

Jeff smiled wide. "I'll say. I'll get you some habanero fries. How's that?"

"That sounds amazing. And a water?"

"Do you like lemonade?" I asked her.

"I do, but water sounds good."

"I'll take a water and a frozen lemonade with two straws." She raised a brow. I grinned. "Trust me."

"I must trust you, I'm here after all."

My heart did a little kick at that before we took the waters and frozen lemonade and went off to the side to wait for our food.

"This place is packed," she said after a moment.

Jeff gestured for us. "I might have pushed you guys to the front of the line," he said with a wink. I shook my head and nodded at a few regulars who had come out for a burger before they went back into the bar for drinks, and probably wings too, knowing them.

"Wow, I guess you get good service here."

"Sometimes. Jeff's a regular too. It works out for us."

"No competition?"

"Not really. We're more symbiotic. Come on, let's go sit over by the fountain there. There's a small table so I don't make a mess of all of this."

"I just realized how messy this is going to be." She popped a fry into her mouth, then her eyes went wide.

"Oh my God, that's hot."

"He loves his habanero. Try it with the lemonade."

I handed over the drink and her lips circled the straw before her cheeks hollowed as she drank.

I, in turn, swallowed hard, thinking about how her lips would look around my cock.

Down boy. One thing at a time. She was a goddamn virgin. A virgin who had made me up to her family as a boyfriend. A fake one.

I needed to have a better handle on everything.

"Come on, come on, eat something else before the top of your head explodes."

"Those were so good though. I don't care that I won't be able to feel my mouth later."

"And that's where he gets you."

We took a seat and dug in. Her eyes rolled to the back of her head, and she groaned so loud, it echoed off the fountain. A couple guys looked over, smirks on their faces, so I glowered at them while doing my best not to adjust myself in my pants. That sound she made went straight to my dick.

"I take it you like it?" I asked, holding back a laugh.

She wiped her mouth daintily and nodded. "Yes, and I promise I don't make sex noises every time I eat." She blushed. "Not that I know what type of noises I make. And I feel like I've said too much. I blame that lemon drop. It was really strong."

"I swear I made it the normal way. But the food should help."

She shook her head and took another bite. After she finished that one, I handed over mine, and she took a bite of the stuffed burger. "Okay, now I don't know which one I like more. Yours is almost more traditional, without the spices."

"It has a kick to it. Yours is like sweet and peppery at the same time. It all balances."

"I'm going to have to work out an extra hour tomorrow for this. It's not great for my arteries."

"No, but you're allowed to indulge every once in a while. It's good for you." I winked as I said it, hoping she caught the double entendre. I wasn't trying to be subtle. "So, what do you do for a living?"

"Is that how you begin to get to know someone?"

"I could ask your favorite color, or where you see yourself in five years. I haven't dated in a while. Even someone I've been with for a year."

She took another bite, then chugged down some water because those fries were spicy as fuck. "I work in PR for a firm and subsidiary. In other words, my bosses move money, make money, and try to help society, and I put the spin on it."

"And are you good at it?" I asked, snacking on a ranch fry.

"Sometimes I think so. I really love my boss. She moved here a couple years ago and began the business right away. She's brilliant at expanding small businesses that want to reach out into other parts of Colorado, and even into Wyoming, but want to keep that small-business feel."

"So does she buy up properties or businesses?"

"Not exactly, it's more of a fifty-fifty symbiotic thing, like you and your food truck."

"That's good. Big business without being too big."

"That's my job. Plus, she owns a matchmaking company. It's kind of interesting how it all works, though none of the staff uses the matchmaking company. At least none of my friends on the staff."

"So, how does that help showing off the goods if you don't trust it?"

"It's not that; it's more that I was so focused on work, and building my own career, that finding a boyfriend wasn't really on top of my priorities."

"And then your family decided to make it a priority."

She rolled her eyes as she snacked on the fries, but the spice didn't seem to bother her. Damn it, she was beautiful. "Yes, and it's just weird because usually they stay out of my business. Which I know is strange to say because it didn't look like it earlier. But they do give me space. They just want me to be as happy as they are. All five of them are married with kids. And I guess I'm next in line since the rest are still teenagers."

"Talk about an age gap."

"Exactly. I know as soon as the next set get out of

college, that matchmaking will begin, but I really didn't want any part of it. I don't know, it's weird."

"I can see how it is. I'm the big brother though, so I sort of want to take care of all of my family's problems, even though they don't always let me."

"You can't take care of everyone's problems, but you can help if they ask."

"We're not good at asking," I said.

She met my gaze and nodded. "I get it. I guess you *are* the big brother. I'm the perpetual middle. I'm not very good at trying to solve everyone's problems, because I'm trying to solve my own. Or at least lie about them." She wiped her hands on the paper napkin. "I still can't believe I lied about you. And you went along with it."

That blush looked damn good on her skin, but that couldn't be the only reason I wanted to know more about her. "It was an interesting night. It's a story."

"And it's embarrassing. At least my family's not worried about me being the sad virgin anymore," she said before blushing hard. "Okay, I can't blame it on the alcohol this time. I can't believe I just said that."

"I really don't mind you talking about that. Though I don't know a lot of women in their twenties that are virgins anymore. Not that there's anything wrong with either," I added quickly. It wasn't as if I'd ever had this kind of conversation before. Devney was all new experiences, it seemed.

She waved her hand at me. "I know that virginity is a construct, and it really doesn't matter if you hold it or not. I think it's more of the idea that I've never been with anyone. I have no idea why I'm telling you about this."

"Because we've been together for a year now."

"See? That just makes me feel even worse."

I reached out and put my hand on hers. She froze, before her chest started to rise and fall rapidly. She didn't look scared. No, she liked my touch.

Good. Because I liked touching her.

"I remember you from that first night. I even talked about you to my friends, to the point that they wanted me to just ask you out even though I didn't see you again. And then just a little bit before you showed up, Ace and I were talking about you, and how I needed to put myself out there. Because the girl that I remembered from just a brief conversation, she wasn't real. I needed to move on. And then you showed up."

She stared at me, wide-eyed. "You're lying. There's no way you remember me."

"Of course, I remember you, Devney. You remembered me."

She was silent for long enough that I was afraid I'd said too much. "What do we do?" she asked softly.

"Now, we're on our first date. A first real date. You're not really lying to your family anymore."

"I guess that's a good thing. So, you want to, what,

continue to date so I'm not a liar?" she asked, the humor in her tone mixed with wariness. I didn't blame her.

"Maybe. And maybe I just want to see what happens."

"I don't know what I want, Heath. But I do know that I'm having a really fun time tonight."

"Yeah? Me too. And don't worry, when you realize that this isn't exactly what you want, you can walk away. But, for now, it's just for fun."

Her eyes widened, and I couldn't help it. I leaned forward and brushed my lips against hers. She closed her eyes, and I slid my tongue against her lips. When she opened for me, I held back a groan, aware that we weren't alone out here, even though nobody was watching us, everyone paying attention to their own dates and food. I just needed to touch her, needed to kiss her.

"You taste amazing," I whispered as I pulled back, licking my lips.

She tasted of spice and sweetness and tartness. And something that was all Devney. Tonight didn't seem fucking real at all.

"Oh," she said as she put her hand to her lips. "I was not expecting that."

"I'm not sure if I should be flattered or not."

She shook her head. "Nothing about tonight makes any sense, but wow."

"Good. I can keep you speechless. Now that I fed you, and kissed you, we're one step closer to us not being a lie."

"I just told them that you were a good time," she said with a laugh. "Which sounds ridiculous. That we were taking it slow and that's why you never came around."

I shrugged. "I can do that. If you need it to be real, we can make it real. I don't know, Devney. I feel like tonight happened for a reason. And I hate fate. I don't believe in it."

"Same. I don't believe in fate at all. But I do believe in these fries." She quickly took a bite and I laughed, knowing that things had gotten a little too serious too quickly.

I sat back and stole a fry, letting the spice hit me. I didn't know how this would end, or if I wanted it to. So for now, I was just going to look at her and listen to her laugh.

And wonder what she meant by a good time.

Chapter Four

Denvey

Light slid against my eyelids, waking me up right before my alarm went off. I rubbed my temples and slowly rolled over to turn off my alarm before it would blare in my ears.

I rolled to my back and let out of breath, knowing that though I slept well for a few hours, I still hadn't gotten enough sleep. It had taken me far too long to relax, and to come to terms with the fact that I might be not-so-fake dating my imaginary boyfriend.

I screamed into my pillow.

We had gone on one date. If you could call dinner from a food truck near a fountain a date. It was more an explanation of the lies that I'd told. I needed to come clean to my family. I knew that. Yes, they would be angry with me, but worse, they would feel bad for making me stressed out at all. And that I couldn't do. I loved my family from the bottom of my heart. And I didn't want them to worry about me.

The problem was, that was all they did.

And because I had made up a boyfriend that turned out to be a very real man, here I was, sitting in my own confusion.

I didn't know what I was supposed to do. Or even if I was doing the right thing, but there was no going back now. That much I knew.

I needed to get to work and go through the thousand things on my list. But first, breakfast and coffee with my best friend. And I had a feeling as soon as she saw my face, she would know something was up. I wasn't going to be able to lie to her. I'd never been able to. It was only because she hadn't lived here for the past couple of years that I had been able to hide my imaginary relationship from her.

"I sound like I've lost my mind."

I got ready for the day, trying to focus on my *actual* life, and not whatever dream scenario I just made up.

But Heath *had* kissed me. He'd kissed me and bought me dinner and had lied for me in front of my family. And while the latter might not sound like a good thing, he had done it to protect me from myself.

How was I supposed to act rationally when I wanted to think about what would happen next?

Except things like this didn't happen to me. It was only a good time, like he said. A fake one. Nothing was going to come of it.

My phone buzzed as I got out of the shower, and I wrapped a towel around myself before looking down at the screen.

Addison: Meet you at Latte on the Rocks?

I bit my lip, but I couldn't avoid our favorite coffee shop just because I was stressed.

Me: Give me thirty minutes? Just got out of the shower.

Addison: Sounds good. Can't wait to see you. I feel like it's been ages.

I smiled to myself as I pulled out my moisturizer and began to work on my face.

Addison had moved away to finish the last two years of her graduate school program. It led to an internship for a company that was connected to the one she was working at now. And when that internship and her degree were finished, she moved back to Denver, and I had my best friend back. I hated her being gone for so long, although it made sense. We had both gone to CU, had been roommates in the dorms in Boulder, and then lived together in a small apartment off campus. We were lucky we had been able to find a place at all, because housing in Boulder was ridiculous. Most people were forced to cram together or spend way too much on loans just to be able to afford rent. My parents had been wonderful about making sure I hadn't needed student loans, too. With the loan crisis as it was, it made sense, but they had eleven children. I had done my best to get scholarships, grants, and we all had chosen in-state schools, and done our best to pay our way as much as possible.

So now I wasn't in debt from school, just the choices I made in my personal life.

Me: I'll see you soon. Love you.

Addison: Love you too! *kissing emoji*

I finished getting ready, blowing out my hair, thankful it seemed to do what I wanted it to. It fell in its natural waves without too much frizz, and I knew that I would never be able to live in a climate with humidity. My hair just wouldn't let me.

Whenever I visited places with humidity, like the beach, or went to Texas for a wedding, my hair got huge.

Addison straightened her hair every other day, but she had a little bit more curl to her hair. So, Denver was perfect for us. It was beautiful, had amazing skylines and things to do, and it didn't kill my hair.

My skin was always dry, and I bathed in a vat of lotion, but that was a small price to pay for not having to deal with the hair of beach days.

I grabbed my things for work, double checking that my first meeting wasn't until ten. I only had to work a partial day at the office that day, because we worked four tens rather than five eight hours. My boss, Paisley, was great at making sure that we got work done but didn't require us to always be at our desks to make it happen. Some days I was able to work from home, as long as I didn't have meetings in person. There were a few people who didn't even live in Denver anymore. I enjoyed the socialization of working with people sometimes though, so I kept an office and came in often. But sometimes there was nothing better than working in a tank top and pajama bottoms while trying to figure out the next PR piece for the company. Paisley made that super easy. I loved the matchmaking division of the company, even though I never would go near it. But I really loved the way that we built up small businesses. And we even guided people in expanding their businesses, like with Latte on the Rocks.

It was an up-and-coming coffee shop and bakery that had the best coffee in Denver, even though it was technically in Arvada, Colorado. It also had some of the best pastries and sandwiches—which I had to be careful with, or I would eat until I was overfull.

The company was actually a subsidiary of another one that was famous in downtown Denver. The owners of Taboo Downtown wanted to expand, but in a unique way. Enter the owners of Latte on the Rocks. They needed help figuring out how to expand without overshadowing each other. Paisley had come in as a consultant, and I had been there for the initial PR rollout for the grand opening.

That was when I became friends with Greer and Raven, the owners of Latte on the Rocks.

So, while Paisley's company didn't own any part of the building, we had done consulting. And everything worked out, and now I got coffee on a near daily basis I didn't have to make myself.

Except that now I knew what Greer's brother's lips tasted like.

I hadn't known the two were related when I made him my fake boyfriend; it was just fate's cruel way of making sure I sat in my own lies and realized the consequences of my own actions.

I wasn't sure how I could even face Greer today, but I would. And I would pretend nothing happened. Because, of course, it hadn't.

I hadn't kissed Heath. He hadn't said he wanted to help me with a certain problem. I blushed so hard thinking about that, because there was no way I'd told him I was a virgin. And that I wanted to get rid of my virginity. No, that had been dream Devney. Idiotic Devney.

"Why are you thinking so hard?" a voice said from beside me, and I realized I'd parked and gotten out of my car without realizing it. That was stupid, and I didn't know how my daydreaming had somehow gotten me to this parking lot without hurting anyone. Dear God, I needed to get my head out of the clouds and back into the real world.

52

"I think I just need caffeine," I said as Addison opened up her arms and I hugged her.

Addison was gorgeous. She was taller than me, curvier, and had shoulder-length brown hair that she straightened. She had round cheeks, a little pert nose, and was adorable.

She could also kick anybody's ass in soccer, rugby, and a few other sports.

She worked for a financial company and rubbed shoulders with millionaires every day, as well as dude-bros in her company who thought that she was just a pretty little woman who should be getting them coffee. It wasn't like we were in a new millennium where women could actually hold jobs and be CEOs. I worked with one of the best CEOs out there, and I hated that my best friend didn't have the same work environment as me.

"Okay, let's get you some caffeine, and you can tell me what happened last night."

"What do you mean?" I asked.

"You called on your way to the bar to go save that poor bartender from your family. And then you never updated me. For all I knew, they had taken him out back and beat him. Or maybe they forced you into a wedding by shotgun or something." She paused as she looked at me. "They didn't actually do that, did they? I mean, I love your family. They're amazing. But oh my God, they are so much."

I snorted and shook my head. "I am so sorry I forgot to tell you. It was a long night."

"Exactly how long. Please tell me that it was a long, *long* night." She emphasized the word long, and I burst out laughing, drawing the attention of patrons for a moment before they went back to their coffee and pastries.

"Not that long. But it was interesting."

Before I could elaborate, Greer Cassidy looked over the register, and smiled at us.

"Hey, you two! It's been a couple days since I've seen you. Your usual?"

I blushed and pressed my lips together, wondering how I could face this woman after kissing Heath. Heath must have kissed thousands of women before. He was a bartender, he was sexy. I wasn't his first. No, I didn't even *have* a first. Hell, I really needed to stop thinking about that. And stop thinking about the idea of Heath being part of that.

Addison elbowed me in the side and frowned. "Are you okay?"

"I'm fine," I squeaked. I looked at Greer. "Actually, I'll take the special. That looks good."

"It's a lavender honey latte, and what about a home-made pop-tart?"

"That sounds like exactly the amount of sugar that I need."

"For here or to go?" she asked as she rang it up.

"For here?" I asked Addison, and she nodded.

"We'll do one cup for here, and then we both need to head into our offices, so I'll probably get a cup to go. Though I will take the crème brûlée latte for now."

"Oh, that sounds yummy." I said, my mouth watering.

"You both win there. Whenever you want your second cup, just let me know if you want a repeat, or something different. Don't worry, I've got you handled. And if you are here for lunch, I have sandwiches coming up too."

"Don't tempt me. I'm starving," I said as she handed over my pastry and Addison's lemon poppy seed muffin.

We paid, and Greer gave me an odd look, before Addison finally pulled me back to our table, coffees and pastries in hand. "What is going on? What happened last night?"

"I don't even know if it actually happened or if I'm imagining it."

"Talk to me."

I looked over my shoulder, seeing that Greer had gone back to the kitchen and Raven was working the front counter. I leaned over our coffees and whispered furiously. By the time I was done, Addison was staring at me, wide-eyed.

"I cannot even believe everything I just heard. You told him you were a virgin?" she asked, her voice low.

She might have whispered, but I still looked around, checking if someone could overhear. "There's nothing wrong with that."

"There's absolutely nothing wrong with you being a virgin. Just like there's nothing wrong if you want to stay that way or do something about it. But he wants to *do* something about it, doesn't he?"

I knew I was blushing. "Stop it. This is so embarrassing."

"Are you kidding me? With how many hours I work, this is literally the best thing that's ever happened to me."

I snorted. "It isn't even happening to you."

Addison smiled as she leaned back in her chair. "It sure as hell feels like it. So, are you going to see him again?"

"Of course not," I said quickly. "He was just being nice."

My best friend raised a single brow, clearly unimpressed with my rationalization. "He kissed you. And bought you a burger."

"The best burger of my life, but he just felt sorry for me. And I'm okay with that," I added quickly, before she could comment. "I'm really okay with it. I'll figure out what I want to do with my life at some point. But I'm perfectly okay not seeing him again. That way I never have to worry about the fact that I lied to my family. I'll tell them it really didn't work out this time."

"Really? That's your plan?"

I froze, that deep voice hitting me far too hard. Addison's eyes widened as she slowly set down her coffee cup. "He's not behind me, is he?" I asked softly.

Addison nodded dramatically, eyes widening further than I thought possible.

"Yes, Devney. I'm right behind you."

"Like in a serial killer sense?" Addison asked before she cleared her throat and looked up at the man of my dreams and nightmares. "Hi, I'm Addison. You must be the figment of Devney's imagination," she said.

I flipped her off. "Really?"

"What? He's a really hot figment of your imagination." She looked back over my shoulder. "It's nice to meet you. I'm Devney's best friend."

"Hello. I'm Devney's fake boyfriend."

I put my hand over my face and groaned into my palms. When Addison's phone started to buzz off the table, I looked up at her and frowned.

"Really?"

"There he goes again."

"Trouble?" Heath asked, ever the white knight. I wanted to hate him a little bit for that, but it looked like he wanted to fix this for Addison, even though he had no idea what *it* was, just like he wanted to fix my screw-ups with my family.

And possibly my virginity.

"It's just work. You know, the usual." Addison drained the last of her coffee and scooped up her things. "I need to head into the office. Apparently, they can't do anything without me." She rolled her eyes and then held out her hand for Heath. "It's lovely to meet you. Please don't hurt my girl. And I want to hear all the details." She winked at me before she headed out, leaving me alone with my not-so-fake boyfriend—and his sister. In his sister's place of business.

I looked around for a crevice to open up and take me to hell. That would be much safer than here.

Heath took Addison's seat across from me. "Hello there."

"Hi. Well. I should have known I would see you when I came here, but I kind of hoped I wouldn't, since I hadn't seen you here before."

Heath grinned at me and shook his head. When he rubbed his hands over his beard, I swallowed hard, wanting those hands on me. I really needed to get laid or something.

From the way his eyes darkened as he looked at me, I had a feeling he knew exactly where my mind went.

"I'm usually here a little bit later. Bartender's hours. But I had to drop off something for Greer. She's in the back about to take a break with her men. And then I saw you sitting here, talking about me. It was fate."

"Or karma being cruel. I'm not quite sure which," I

said, before sipping my coffee. All I could taste was my own fear and anxiety. Was I sweating? I felt like I was sweating.

"So."

"So."

"You gave me your number. I was going to call you today."

I wanted to believe that, but the last guy I had given my real number to hadn't called me. Guys didn't call me. I was used to that. I was not used to whatever the hell was going on with Heath.

"Oh. That's okay."

"I'm not done with you, Devney."

The way he said that, with that deep growl? Damn it. I had to press my thighs together. I still had to go into work and act like I knew what the fuck I was doing.

"Oh. That's good."

Oh. My. God.

That was what I said? I was an intelligent independent businesswoman, and yet poof. There went the brain cells.

"Unless you want me to be done with you, and then we'll see." He shrugged as he said it, looking far too growly and sexy for his own good.

"I don't know if I want you to be done with me?" I paused. "I can't believe I just said that out loud and in such a high squeaky voice."

He grinned, his eyes brightening. Damn it, he was good-looking.

"I want more." He paused, and I let out a shaky breath. "Let's have fun. We'll make that lie a reality."

My mouth went dry, and my knees went weak—and I was still sitting down. I swallowed and nodded. "Okay. So, I guess like you said. A good time, whatever that means?"

He leaned forward, and since it was a small table, I could feel the heat of him. I licked my lips. I hadn't meant to, but when his gaze went straight to my lips, and narrowed as he looked back up at me, I knew I was in trouble.

Good trouble.

"Oh yes, we'll have a good time. I'll make sure of it."

He leaned forward and wiped the foam from my chin before he stood up, slid his thumb into his mouth, and walked out of the café, leaving me sitting there, slightly damp, slightly embarrassed, and far more confused than I ever thought possible.

Chapter Five

Heath

I still didn't know what I had been thinking, but there was no going back now. I'd thought about Devney since the first time I had seen her. The first minute she walked into the bar, I had about lost my damn mind. We had spoken one word to each other, maybe two. And she smiled, and then gone off with what I had to assume now was one of her siblings. I'd told Ace about her. Just an instance where you remember someone that made you smile, that tweaked a certain interest. But nothing was ever supposed to come from that. Nothing ever did. And yet here I was, on my way to pick her up for our date. I offered to pick her up or meet her at the head of the trail, unsure what she would prefer. After all, I didn't want to seem like a creeper. If she didn't want me knowing where she lived, I wouldn't. But she had rattled off her address, and now I was on my way to see her.

Even if this was the last time I would see her, I would deal. This was just casual, fun. A quick hike that was a date. Because I was her fake not-fake boyfriend. Whatever the hell that meant.

I was just her good time, and I was fine with that.

I shook my head as I pulled into her driveway, noticing the small ranch house with large windows and a cute porch. She had a rocker in the front, though no cushions. I didn't blame her, because the weather in Colorado was odd enough that it could rain one minute and be sunny the next. Cushions didn't stand a chance.

I got out of the car and made my way to the front door. She opened it before I got halfway there and waved.

"I saw you on my doorbell camera. I have it set so I can see whoever goes near my driveway and it alerts me. Which isn't great whenever the neighborhood kids like to ride their bikes in my driveway, but I digress." She let out a deep breath, and grinned. "Sorry. I'm talking really fast."

I smiled and gestured towards her hiking boots.

"You're dressed for the occasion though. You look good." I leaned down and brushed my lips against hers. This was a date. We were making her lies real. When she shivered, smiling softly against my lips, I figured I'd made the right choice.

"Hi," she said and sighed softly. "That was nice. And

thank you. They're old hiking boots, so they're broken in. I have another set of boots that I need to break in, but I figured getting blisters today and whining about it wouldn't be very fun."

"True, but you need to break them in some time."

"I just walk around my house with extra socks on. Not the most exciting way to spend an evening, but it works."

"Pretty much. I remember the first time my brothers and I went on a hike, and my youngest brother hadn't broken in his shoes yet. Let's just say he cursed us out."

"What did your sister say about that?" she asked as she got in the car. I frowned, wondering how to explain that. It was always awkward to bring up that we hadn't been raised with our sister.

I moved around the car and got in on my side, starting the engine.

"That was during the years Greer wasn't living with us."

She frowned as I moved us down the street and out of the neighborhood to get on the highway. There were tons of trails all around West Denver, and it was super easy to find a trailhead and hike without needing a permit. We wouldn't be hiking for long, but I did have a backpack of snacks and water. Just enough to enjoy ourselves.

"What do you mean?" she asked.

"Well, since it is our second date I should get into the details."

"Second? Oh my," she said with a laugh, and I grinned.

"Moving fast," I said quickly. "My parents didn't have the most typical relationship."

"I'm sorry."

"Don't be. I mean, there's nothing you can do about it. My parents suck. They still do. Not the greatest thing for a son to say, but they do. The first time that they got divorced, it was right after I got healthy."

I cursed, realizing I had started their story in the wrong part.

She frowned at me as I sighed.

"Long story even longer. When I was a kid, I had non-Hodgkin's lymphoma."

"Heath, I'm so sorry. I'm glad you're okay now. I mean, you are okay now, right?"

I nodded and gripped her hand. I watched the long lines of her throat as she swallowed. She was so damn beautiful, and it made it hard to think. Hell, it just made me hard.

"I am fine. Seriously. Yes, it sucked. I had to go through chemo and all the things you do when cancer's trying to kick your ass, but non-Hodgkin's lymphoma, even in children, is treatable. My lymph nodes were swollen, and it sucked, and it hurt. I don't even remember the first time they started to hurt. I just remember my mom getting really scared, and my parents fighting. I had a bone marrow biopsy, which I remember hurt like hell. And then we did chemotherapy, but we didn't need to do radiation. Because I didn't have complications and things worked out and I didn't need anything extra, it was relatively easy compared to some of my friends in the hospital with me."

I turned down the highway, facing the majestic Rockies, reminding me that I was settled, that I was here. That I wasn't that scared little boy anymore.

"That must have been a lot for your whole family."

"It was. My baby sister and brother were far too young to understand what was going on, hell, I was too young to understand what was going on. I just knew it hurt and I was tired and I was throwing up all the time. And my twin really didn't know what was going on, either."

"I didn't know you had a twin."

"Yeah, August. Luca's the youngest, Greer's right above him. And then it's me and August. We're identical, but we don't do anything alike. He's a nerdy chemistry teacher who is brilliant, and a jock, and was the quarterback of our football team. He got a full ride to our university just on academics alone, and he could have played sports in college if he hadn't been going for dual degrees."

"August does sound pretty amazing."

I reached over and tapped her nose before I turned down the street towards the trailhead.

"You're with this twin here. Just making sure you

know."

"Oh, I do."

"I went to college too, but for business. It was a little harder for me, but August was always there to help, and made sure I always passed."

"You didn't like trade spaces in classes, did you?"

I laughed. "No, we couldn't really do that, not till we were older. And then we ended up having different beards. When we were kids though, you could always tell us apart because I was skinnier, a little sicklier." I shrugged it off as if I couldn't remember, but I could. And I was fine.

We got out of the car after I parked and made our way down the trail, not hand in hand, but close enough that our hands brushed against one another.

"Anyway, I was fine, August was fine, the rest of us were fine. My parents were not."

"A child being hurt or any huge trauma like that tests a marriage."

"Yes, it does. And it sucks. Because my parents decided that they were better off separate, but they didn't want to keep us together."

"They split you up?" she asked, her voice raised enough that birds flew out of the trees. She flinched, but I sighed and gripped her hand as we kept moving, mostly so that she wouldn't trip over the rock in front of her. And because I liked touching her. I didn't let go.

"Our dad decided to take the boys, and my mom took Greer. And we moved a lot. Greer moved more than us, Mom always going from job to job."

"They parent-trapped you?" she asked, her voice so aghast, I just squeezed her hand.

"Pretty much. And then they got married again."

"And you got to live with your baby sister."

"Yep. For a few years. At least until we hit high school, and then they got divorced again."

"And they split you up again."

"Yep. Mom took her away, and they made it so we couldn't even contact each other. We tried to email and call, but the guilt from the other parent when we got caught was too much. And it got weird. Greer was our baby sister, but we rarely saw her, and we didn't get to know her. I didn't get to growl at her first boyfriend or watch her get ready for prom. I didn't get to help her learn how to drive, I didn't get to do any of that."

"But she has you now. I mean, you moved out here for her, right?"

I nodded. "Our parents are on marriage three, and on a honeymoon around the world that should take at least another year, thank God." I rolled my eyes as I said it.

We came to the bluff. It was gorgeous, the trees parting so you could see the edge of the cliff and a small stream trickling through.

She pulled out her phone to take a photo.

"Enough about me and my sad story."

"One more thing on it though." She looked up at me and smiled. I swallowed hard, reminding myself this was just a fake date.

"You're here now for her. You're here with all of your family. And in the end, that's the only thing that matters."

I pushed her hair back from her face before I took her phone from her hand.

"Yeah. That's part of it." Then I leaned down and kissed her, snapping a selfie before she could say anything.

She laughed as she pulled away and took the phone back from me.

"How did you center us so you could see the background so wonderfully?"

"Pure luck," I said with a laugh, then looked down at the photo. You could see the mountains in the background, the trees surrounding the frame, my lips on Devney's in the center.

Cheesy as fuck, but damn if it didn't make me smile.

We kept on hiking, and we decided to no longer discuss anything too heavy. I hadn't even meant to bring up my family, or the fact that I'd been sick as a kid. I didn't like thinking about my parents. All I wanted to think about was the family that was here now. They were the ones that mattered.

We made our way to the end of the trail, and Devney was panting a bit, her chest rising up and down, so I did my best not to stare at her nipples through her shirt. But it wasn't easy. Especially when she pushed her hair back from her face, pressing her breasts against my arm.

I leaned down and trailed my finger along her collarbone.

Her lips parted and she sucked in a breath before I leaned down to take her mouth again.

"Let's get you some water. You look parched."

"Oh?" she asked, before she wrapped her arms around my neck and pulled me closer. I wrapped my arms around her waist, pressing her body against mine. She was soft and supple and I wanted to take those shorts off and see exactly how she felt against me. The kiss deepened and she groaned. I rocked against her and realized that I was hard as fuck, pressing my dick against her stomach.

She panted as I slid my hand into her hair, tugging gently. She moaned, and I deepened the kiss before someone cleared their throat behind me. I cursed, backing away. Thankfully, Devney stood in front of me, blocking my erection, as a man with a walking stick, large backpack, and wide grin looked at us.

"Thanks for the show, but you're kind of blocking the walkway."

"Sorry," Devney burst out, and I put my hand on her shoulder and nodded at the man.

"No problem. Enjoy your walk."

"Probably not as much as you kids will," the man said,

He chuckled under his breath and walked past us, whistling a tune I didn't recognize.

"Well," Devney whispered under her breath. "I'm mortified."

"I'm not. Of course, if he hadn't shown up, we'd probably be in the bushes there, and I'd be taking care of your virginity with my bare ass in the air and rocks on my knees."

I had probably said the wrong thing, but she burst out laughing and tugged on my hand.

"When I think about sex, the outdoors doesn't really factor in. I mean, we could check for ticks, but I would rather not do that with your dick inside me."

I nearly tripped over my feet at her words. "Look at you, using all the dirty words," I said while laughing.

"I can use dirty words; I know the dirty words and I like them. Just because I haven't had sex doesn't mean I don't know how to get myself off. Thank you very much."

I groaned and adjusted myself.

"Let's get you home. Because damn it, it's getting hard to think."

We stood at the car door, and she slid her hand down my chest, and even further down. When she cupped me over my jeans, I groaned.

"You're playing with fire, baby girl."

"Let's go back to my place. You know, just to check for ticks."

I groaned again and rocked in her hand.

"We could do that. If you want."

There was a moment of silence where I swore the earth stood still, and you couldn't even hear the wind blow through the trees.

Her answer could change everything.

"Let's go," she whispered.

I kissed her again, but knew it wasn't time. Not when I could see the hesitation in her gaze. We'd started this on a dare of sorts, and that meant I'd have to step back.

I leaned back and kissed her forehead. "I wouldn't mind kissing you for a long time yet, Devney. Then we can plan our next date."

She licked her lips. "Yeah?"

"Yeah. Though I'm not sure if I want that one to be fake."

She grinned and shook her head. "No, probably not. Because those kisses didn't feel fake." She looked down pointedly between us. "Neither does that."

I shook my head. "Yeah, I'm going to need to take a breath or eight before I drive or I'll run us into a ditch."

"That would suck." She let out a breath, that worry finally receding. "Thank you for today. I've had fun. It's been a long time since I just had fun."

I kissed her again. I couldn't help it. "With the move and setting up the bar, honestly, same. Let's get you home, get you fed, and we can plan the next date."

"And I'll figure out how to tell my family that I'm a horrible person." She cringed as she said it and I winced for her.

"You're not a horrible person."

"I lied. I'm *still* lying. I don't like it and I need to fix it."

"Sure. I can see that. But maybe they'll understand if you tell them *why* you did it."

She looked past me into the foothills and nodded, though I wasn't sure if I believed her. "I need to do that too."

Then she looked at me and smiled so brightly I nearly fell to my knees. There was something about this woman that changed things and it should worry me. Because I was a gruff asshole most of the time. I had to be most of the time with my job, even when I wasn't playing the affable bartender as I was still the boss in charge and keeping my people safe. But with her? I didn't want to be. And that was probably a problem.

"Let's get you home," I said a bit gruffer than intended.

She smiled and got into the car. I closed the door behind her and leaned against the metal for a moment, taking a deep breath.

I was in trouble.

So much trouble.

Chapter Six

Devney

M y body still tingled from the weekend before, and it wasn't as if I hadn't had a mountain of things to do since then. I had made out with Heath Cassidy in public, and there wasn't anything fake about it. I wanted him.

Wanted him more than I probably should.

However, my life did not revolve around Heath, my loins, or the fact that I wanted him. I had a job, a career, and a family who was still worried about me, not to mention the guilt that crept into every conversation I had with them.

I would tell them. It was wrong that I hadn't. All of my little white lies had turned into one dark lie that had changed everything. Maybe it had made something for the better, but that didn't mean it was a smart thing to do. I needed to tell my family. I needed to be brave enough.

As if she knew I was thinking about her, my phone rang and I saw my mom's name.

I smiled and answered quickly. Because even if she could be slightly overbearing, she wanted what's best for me and was my mom. My everything.

"Hi, Mom."

"Hello, baby. Are you alone?" she asked, and I barely resisted the urge to roll my eyes. She couldn't see me since it wasn't a video call, but I swear she always knew when I was sassing her, even through a phone. I might be in my twenties now, a full adult, but I was still her baby girl.

"I'm alone. I'm actually getting ready to go meet Addison."

"Oh, where are you going?"

Even though the answer wouldn't be a lie, she would probably see a little too much into it.

"I'm on my way to Lost and Found."

"To see Heath?"

"Maybe. But it was actually Addison's idea to go there because she wanted their special."

"Oh, those avocado egg roll things that I heard about?"

I frowned. "How do you know about the avocado egg rolls?"

My mom cleared her throat, and I groaned.

"Please tell me that you and William didn't go to the

bar to check out Heath. It's bad enough the five older siblings decided to make a scene about it."

"We didn't go. Maureen mentioned it." She paused long enough I knew that the next blow was coming. "She and Brian went."

I groaned again because I knew this was only the beginning.

"Why did Maureen and her husband go to the bar? I assume it was on a weekday? What about the kids?"

"It was their date night. Elizabeth and Ashley babysat."

Elizabeth was my second oldest stepsibling, and Ashley was her wife. They had two kids of their own, and everybody always babysat each other's kids. They didn't usually need an actual sitter, unless the entire family was going out without the kids. Which had only happened once.

"Okay, I'm going to go call Maureen and yell at her. The family does not need to go stalk that bar. Or Heath."

"We just want to get to know your boyfriend. I mean, they left him alone for a whole year."

Guilt ate at me, but a phone conversation with just my mom was not the time to bring up the fact that I had made up an imaginary boyfriend so they would get off my back. If anything, it was now worse, but there was no coming back from that.

At least not right now.

"Please tell Maureen to leave it be. And I will do the same. In fact, tell everybody. I guess I'm just lucky enough that the younger kids aren't old enough to get in."

"Oh, they are. They just can't be served alcohol. It's not a twenty-one and over club. They serve food. Including those avocado egg rolls I want to try."

Now my mouth was watering thinking about those avocado egg rolls. I was going to have to try them tonight, but still, this wasn't over.

"Mom. I love you all. But you guys need to give me some space. I know you want me to be happy, and I am. I love my job. I love my friends. Addison's back in town."

"I know, baby. I'm so glad she's back. Because when you didn't have her, you just had us. And while we are many, I want you to have friends. I want you to be happy. I love you." She paused, and I swallowed hard, knowing my mom was wiping away tears. She was emotional and loving. While my family was slightly overbearing, okay a lot overbearing, they loved me. But they were far too much for me. Hence why I had made up a boyfriend.

"I know that when I married William, things changed. It was just the three of us for so long. And when we lost your dad, it was the two of us and we had to figure out life on our own. But your dad loved you so much. Just like I do."

I sat down at the end of my bed, playing with the shoes on the ground near me. I had been in the process of deciding between heels and flats for the evening, and now I just wanted to curl up and hold my mom.

Because while I had lost my father, she had lost her husband. And yet she put me first always. Even when she found William.

"William is the best stepdad ever. And he never begrudged me the fact that I didn't want to change my name. That I wanted to keep a part of Dad. I get that he's amazing. And the top five, they never looked at me as anything other than their sister. They never begrudged me the fact that I didn't look like them, I didn't have their last name, or I was the new baby of the family."

"Of course not. You are family. Even with a different last name. Womack is still my middle name though, you know."

"I do. Although Alice Womack Johnson is a bit long."

"Alice Marie Womack Johnson. Thankfully I just use initials when I'm signing papers, but the longer papers that need everything official? It takes me hours." She joked.

"I do need to head out and meet Addison. It's her night off."

"And since your boyfriend owns a bar, I guess weekends are pretty much filled with that?"

I cleared my throat, because again, the lies came back to bite me in the ass. I needed to do better. I needed to be better.

And I would.

Once I figured out what to say.

"We went hiking last weekend. He doesn't have to close every night, they have a full staff, and his co-owner Ace does it too. They alternate. I think he actually works fewer hours than I do sometimes during my campaigns."

My mom laughed on the other end of the line. "That doesn't actually fill me with confidence since my baby girl works twenty hours a day."

I heard the sarcasm, so I rolled my eyes. "Not too many. Paisley doesn't work me hard."

"Not sure about that, but I know that young lady works even harder than you do."

"Yes, she does. And we're a good team. Just like me and Addison."

"I hope that you have fun tonight. Maybe more fun than you usually have," she said with a laugh, and I rolled my eyes again. "And maybe get Paisley out of the office. I know she runs that matchmaking company, but seriously, my girls need to start dating. Although you have Heath, and when you finally bring him around we can decide if he's good enough for you."

"Mom, there is so much wrong with that statement, I don't even know where to begin."

"True, but I'm old school here, let me have my match-making mama abilities. There's eleven of you, you know. I worry."

"And we aren't in Regency England where you have to marry us off like cattle before we hit the ripe old age of twenty-five."

"Well, you are twenty-four. But you do have prospects, and a dowry."

I rolled my eyes again even though she couldn't see me.

"I'm headed out. After I pick my shoes."

"Do the heels. Your legs look great in them. Don't bother with flats. You can wear flats and other shoes that support your arches when you're older."

"Thanks for the fashion advice. I love you."

"I love you, too. Now bring that boy around for dinner one day. As long as you say it might happen, I can fend off the wolves." The wolves being the rest of the family.

I knew there was no way to get out of this. "I'll think about it. How about that?"

"That's better than the no that you usually say. It sounds promising. Have fun and make good choices."

"Thanks, Mom," I said, teasing. I hung up and decided to take her advice and wear high heels. I could protect my arches later. Or put my feet in an ice bath if I rolled my ankle like an idiot.

I took a rideshare to the bar just because I was planning on having at least two drinks, and met Addison at the front door.

"Hey, you," my best friend said as she opened up her

arms. I wrapped my arms around her and hugged her tight. Her shoulder-length dark hair was straightened, as usual, and it framed her face perfectly. She also had on tight black pants, and a crop top thing that had a see-through layer on top so that way it was still a full shirt, but she showed a lot of skin.

"Look at you. Very sexy."

She looked down at my baby-blue dress that covered my chest completely and ended in cap sleeves, but was super short and showed off my back.

"You're showing off legs for days. Spin for me."

I rolled my eyes but spun for her. She wolf whistled and caught the eyes of a couple guys walking past.

"Okay. This is going to be fun. I can't wait to see Heath again."

"Seriously?"

"I'm just saying. It'll be nice to get to know the man you made up."

"Stop. If you say that out loud, I swear one of my siblings will just pop up. Did you know that Maureen and her husband came and ate here this week apparently?"

"Oh my God, they're relentless. You're really going to have to tell them."

"I know. I just feel so silly."

"It's going to suck and they're going to be angry, but then they may realize how overbearing they are when it comes to your relationship status. I mean, they're overbearing about my relationship status, and I'm not even related to you."

We made our way inside and found a booth, and I pointedly didn't look at the bar.

"I don't see the bearded man. I see another one, but as his arm is around a voluptuous woman and she's wearing an engagement ring, I assume that's Ace and his fiancée?"

I looked over and nodded, oddly grateful that it wasn't Heath kissing another woman. Not that I knew if we were exclusive or not. Or anything actually. This was what happens when you lie. You end up in complicated situations where you feel like there is no out.

"Heath isn't here. At least not right now. I cannot believe we're here without telling him. Now I feel like a stalker."

"You can text him."

"I will. In a minute. Once I get a drink in me."

Before the waitress came over, I noticed a woman with long curly red hair at the bar sipping a martini by herself, gorgeous legs crossed, her stiletto heels tapping the metal pole at the bottom of the bar as a footrest.

I knew that woman.

"Paisley's here."

"Oh really? Tell her to come over. Unless she's waiting on someone. I haven't seen her in forever. You go, I'll save the booth."

"Okay."

"And what do you want to drink?"

I waved and shook my head. "I don't know. A lemon drop?"

"I can do that. Or see if there's something on special?"

"Perfect."

I made my way over to Paisley, wondering if I was interrupting her, but there was such a sad expression on her face, I couldn't leave her alone.

"Paisley?" I asked, my voice soft.

She turned to me with wide eyes, before she put a fake smile on her face. "Devney! Oh wow. Small world. Big city though. I didn't know you'd be here."

"Addison and I are here for a drink and some appetizers. Do you want to join us?"

Paisley winced and looked around. "Well, since my date is an hour late, I'm pretty sure I just got stood up. So yes. I'd love to join you. If you don't mind that I'm going to order a second martini right after I'm finished with this one."

"Are you serious? He didn't text or call or anything?"

"Nope. He didn't. And, well, that's just par for the course. I finally put myself out there after the divorce, and the guy doesn't even show up." She leaned over the bar. "I'm going to join them at my booth, can I pay my tab real quick?"

Ace smiled at me, lifting his chin, before he turned to Paisley.

"I caught the tail end of that, so your drink's on me."

Paisley grimaced. "I really don't need a pity martini."

"Tip your server well on your second one, and we'll call it even. Seriously, the guy doesn't deserve you."

"He really doesn't," Ace's fiancée said, and Paisley smiled, with a little brittleness attached.

"Well, thank you."

"Good to see you, Devney. Heath should be right out."

I blushed as Paisley raised a brow, but then I couldn't think of anything to say. Because Heath was there, walking out, his gaze right on mine. I pressed my thighs together as Paisley cursed beneath her breath beside me.

That must have caught Heath's attention, because he turned to her, eyes wide.

"Paisley?" he asked, the surprise in his voice nearly knocking me off my heels.

They knew each other? Wait, she had just said ex-husband. Was this him? No, that's way too small a world. And yet, what did I know about Heath? What did I know about Paisley?

I really wanted to go back to my seat with Addison.

As if I had called to her, Addison was beside me, hand in mine as she whispered in my ear, "Everything okay? The waitress is saving our booth."

I didn't say anything, I just stared between Paisley and Heath who both looked as if they had seen ghosts.

"I didn't know you lived here," Paisley said, her voice cool.

"Yeah. We moved here a year ago."

Paisley stiffened again. "We?"

Heath gave me an apologetic look before he cleared his throat.

"Yeah, Paisley. All of us. The whole Cassidy family."

And then it clicked, Paisley's middle name.

Paisley *Cassidy* Renee.

"So, you two know each other?" I asked after a moment. Heath looked at Paisley before coming around the bar towards me. Paisley stiffened and tried to get out of her seat, but it was difficult in her pencil skirt. It felt as if it took forever for Heath to get there.

"Yeah, from back in Portland."

Paisley laughed and downed the rest of her drink.

"He's my ex-brother-in-law. I used to be married to his twin."

Relief and an odd sense of foreboding slammed into me. Paisley was not Heath's ex, but she was connected. Well, damn it. It really was a small world.

"So August lives here now?" Paisley added, shaking her head.

"Yes. We all do. We didn't know you were living here, Paisley. Greer moved here first, so we came after her."

Something sad crossed over Paisley's face before she smiled. "Good. Good to know that you guys are getting closer to Greer after all this time. I didn't know this was your bar, Heath. I wouldn't have come. I don't want to make things awkward. Especially because from the way you two are looking at each other, there seems to be a connection between you and my head of PR."

"Oh, well, yes," I said, my voice trailing off, as Heath cleared his throat.

"Devney and I are seeing each other. She hasn't met the rest of the family. Though she does know Greer."

"Well, that makes one of us," she mumbled, and I wondered what had gone on between August and Paisley, but it wasn't my business.

Paisley sighed before she smiled brightly. It almost reached her eyes. "Everything's fine. August and I didn't break each other's hearts. I promise. Right?" She looked at Heath, who stood there expressionless.

"Anyway, since everyone around here knows I was just stood up, and now with a blast from my past, I'm heading home. Don't worry, I'm going to rideshare. Have fun and I'll see you at work." She noticed Addison for the first time. "You must be Addison, Devney's best friend. It's wonderful to meet you. I wish it could be longer and under better circumstances, but I'm literally going to run out of here if that's okay with you." And she finally scooted off the bar stool and made her way out, leaving a wake of confusion.

"Wow. I love your boss, but this is like a freaking soap

opera. Are you okay?" she asked, and I looked to see that she was asking Heath. I loved my best friend for that.

"Yeah. I just didn't expect her to be living in Denver. Fuck. I'm going to have to tell August."

"Was it actually a good breakup?" I asked, not sure if it was my business.

"I have no idea. One day he was married, the next day he wasn't. I didn't ask what happened because he wouldn't let me. We might be twins, but that doesn't mean I'm allowed to pry. August is more closed off than the other siblings." He sighed and shook his head. "I have to get back to work, but how about I make sure you get what food you want, and I'll visit in a bit, if you're still up for it? It's good to see you here by the way." He leaned forward and brushed his lips against mine.

Addison sighed sweetly and murmured, "Well, hello."

Heath cleared his throat. "Oh, sorry. Hi, I'm Heath. It's nice to officially meet you rather than the twenty seconds we had at the coffee place."

Addison reached out to shake his hand. "Hi, I'm Addison, Devney's best friend. And I know all the background information so you don't have to worry that I'm like her siblings. Who I love, but wow. Anyway, we're going to go back to our booth before the waitress thinks we've run off. We'll see you later. Promise."

"What she said," I said with a laugh, feeling far more confused than ever.

Heath grinned and pushed my hair back from my face. "You look amazing, by the way."

"Oh. Well, thanks."

Addison nearly pulled me off my heels and we staggered back to the booth. I was grateful for my drink, and for the avocado egg rolls on the table.

"So, I'm going to need a lot more information," Addison said after a moment.

"Honestly, same. Because wow."

Addison nodded, and as we toasted our drinks, I wondered what exactly just happened.

Chapter Seven

Heath

"Are you heading out?"

I turned to Ace and nodded. "Yeah. You good closing tonight?"

"My girl has a late dinner with the bosses, and then is probably going to head home and pass out after such a long week. I'm fine closing. You go do your family dinner. It's why you're here after all." He winked as he said it, but I still rubbed a hand over my chest wondering why I was so nervous. It had been my idea to move here. My idea to pick up everything and start over in a new state. But my baby sister had done it, and I wanted to get to know her. And it hadn't taken much convincing to get the others on board. After all, they were all just starting off in their careers. And while it had taken a little finagling to get the right qualifications to move their jobs to Colorado, it worked.

And now it was time to get used to the whole family thing.

Meaning a family dinner, where I would try not to solve whatever problems my family had.

"Call me if you need me."

"I'm not going to need you, but don't worry, we know we can always rely on you." Ace gave me a look and cleared his throat. "And your family can count on you too. Don't be so nervous, brother."

I sighed and glared at my friend. "I don't know if I appreciate how well you can read me."

"It just takes practice. Plus, when it comes to your family? You always stress out so I can read your face."

I picked up my things and frowned, nodding at a regular as they came in to sit at the edge of the bar where our other bartender helped them out. "What do you mean always?"

"I mean you lost precious time with Greer, but you have it now. You guys see each other at least once a week. You and your brothers are close as hell, closer than I am with my brothers. Hell, I'm closer to you than my brothers."

"And considering I don't like you, that's saying something." I winked, and he flipped me off.

"See? We act like family, and you're even closer to

your sibs. You were denied a relationship with your little sister growing up, but you have it now. You don't have to fix everything for her. She knows that, and I wish you did." He paused. "In fact, I don't think there's anything to fix. She's happy, getting married to not one but two guys who would burn the world down to protect her. So maybe you can just sit back and be the big brother she needs. Not the protector."

"I'm not sure if I know how to do that."

"Because you're learning, or because you want to be the big growly bear who doesn't want anyone to touch the baby sister?"

"No, she's doing great on her own. I'm just trying to figure out where I fit in her life."

"Heath. You fit where you need to. You're there."

"I just don't want to screw it up. And I want our family to actually figure things out."

"You do dinners and you have holidays together. From where I'm standing, you're already there. And maybe, just maybe, you could settle down with more than just family."

He gave me a pointed look, and I shook my head.

"I'm out."

"Tell Devney hi."

I flipped him off again as a few of our regulars laughed, and made my way out back to my car.

Traffic was light, so it didn't take me long to get home.

I wanted a quick shower and to change my clothes before dinner at Greer's.

It was still odd to me that Greer was in a serious relationship. That she was getting married, and already living with the loves of her life. It didn't faze me that she was with two men. She loved them, and they all loved each other. It was more that I didn't know where I fit in. And that was on me.

My phone buzzed and I looked down at it, a smile spreading over my face before I could think twice about it.

Devney: have fun tonight. By the way, did I leave my jacket in your car?

We had gone out for another date the night before, just a quick appetizer and drink before we both headed back home since we had work to do. Devney worked long hours; the fact that she worked long hours with my ex-sister-in-law still made me jolt. I hadn't told my brother about it. I wasn't sure I should. Or how I could. Again, you would think I hadn't been a big brother my entire life. But when it came to my twin and his relationships, I tried to stay out of it.

But I wasn't always good at it.

Me: yes, it's in my living room now. I can try to drop it off later if you want. Depending on how late dinner goes.

Devney: I don't need it right away, so how about I get it tomorrow when we meet up?

I smiled and wondered why it seemed so natural to see each other so many times during a week. Especially when we were not serious about this. Yet we saw each other at least four or five times a week, and while we had made out, kissed, touched, we still hadn't had sex.

Interesting.

Me: deal. Don't work too hard.

Devney: I'll try. But I'll probably fail.

I smiled and said goodbye, knowing that she would work too hard, so I would take care of her tomorrow. Because I wanted to. Because I needed to.

With that thought, I quickly showered and got dressed, and then jumped into my car and headed towards Greer's.

She lived in a two-story house a couple of neighborhoods away from me. We were all on the west side of Denver, in one of the little suburbs that seemed to combine with another little suburb and so on. I was still getting the lay of the land, but I liked the area. The main streets seemed to be alphabetical, and everything was numbered when you went horizontal. And with the mountains being in the west, you always knew what direction you were going. I wondered how I got around any other city after living in this one only a year.

I parked behind Luca's large SUV, while August had taken the free spot in the driveway. We tried not to block the whole street, considering three people lived in Greer's house plus all of us.

Of course, I knew that both Greer's men, Noah and Ford, each had large families as well. So we would probably take up the entire block or two if we all visited at once. Not that we had done that. We were still taking things slow when it came to the large families, and I felt like that had more to do with my sister and her men than us. It was overwhelming with just the Cassidys, I couldn't imagine adding one thousand others.

I grabbed the bottle of wine I brought with me and headed towards the front door.

When Greer opened it, I grinned and she smiled wide.

"You're here. And you're the last one. Which is odd because you're usually the first."

I stepped inside. "Sorry, I was talking with Ace, time got away from me, and I still wanted to shower. You know, get the bar funk off me." I leaned down and kissed her cheek, then hugged her, relieved when she wrapped her arms around my waist.

"It's okay. Luca just showed up."

"Because a box of kittens made their way here." He pointed at the box, and my eyes widened as five tiny little heads peeked out.

"Well hell," I grumbled, as I went over to Luca and looked down at the box.

"What happened?"

My brother just shrugged, a sad look crossing his features. "Somebody dumped them on our doorstep, and we checked them over but they couldn't stay overnight at the vet office. So they'll stay with me."

"And what about Horatio?" I asked Greer.

"He's in the bedroom. While he would totally get along with the babies and want to take care of them and name them and be the best parent ever, we want to quarantine these little ones."

"Well, they're fricking adorable," I said, as one sniffed at my fingers.

They had their eyes open and were making little meowing sounds as they walked around the box.

They had a small litter box, as well as some food and water inside, and it was a rather big box. They seemed happy.

"What are you going to do with them?" I asked as Luca studied me.

"Are you in the mood for a kitten?"

I winced and shook my head. "No, sadly. You know I'm allergic."

Luca cursed under his breath as August came into the room with both of Greer's men.

"Shit, I forgot."

"We may be twins, but my allergies are notorious."

"You shouldn't even be touching the kittens then," Greer said, pushing me out of the way.

"I'm just slightly allergic. It doesn't close my throat or anything. I already take allergy meds for the pollen and everything outside. I'll go wash my hands and everything will be fine. Promise."

"Still, you come over here and I have a cat here and you don't say anything. How did I not know this?" Sadness edged over her features and I wanted to kick something.

"Damn our parents, just... Just damn them to hell."

"It's okay. Luca forgot too."

"Because I'm an idiot. Sorry. You sure you're going to be all right with a box of fluff balls and dander?"

"I'll be fine. I promise. If it gets too bad, I'll go stand out on the balcony. You guys have a great view." I nodded at both Ford and Noah. "Good to see you two."

"Good to see you. You need a beer?"

I shook my head. "No. I have paperwork to go over tonight. You got any water?"

"Sparkling or flat?"

"Sparkling sounds good. I can pretend it's a soda."

"Oh, so you're stopping soda too?" August asked as he tilted his beer at me.

"Trying. Do you know how hard it is to work at a bar that serves greasy food alongside healthy food? All I want to do all day is snack on wings and drink soda, then end it all with a beer. Kind of hard to stay healthy with that."

"Well, at least you go to the gym and work out. I'm going to have to keep up with you. You know, just so we can stay identical."

August grinned at me, and I shook my head.

"True, but you're going to have to add a few scars."

I said it offhandedly, because we were joking, but something crossed August's face, and I wanted to take it back.

While August had a few scars on his knees from falling when we were little, I still had the scars from my port and surgery. Scars August didn't have because he hadn't had cancer.

I didn't know why I'd even brought it up. Because August was always twitchy when it came to that. I knew he had some form of guilt, this twin thing that didn't make any sense.

But it wasn't like we ever brought it up. Why would I want to bring up the fact that I had been sick as a kid? But August hadn't been sick and I knew that sometimes it was something between us. Though never on my part.

I never felt anger that my twin was never sick. Why would I want to inflict that on another kid? On someone who had my face. Who held part of me. That never made sense to me, but August always was a little weird about it.

Thankfully Greer stepped in and changed the subject.

"Okay, today we are doing cheese plates to start with."

I looked at her, then at Noah, who just shrugged.

"Sorry, it's a cheese house. It's what we do."

"Well, thankfully we're not lactose intolerant," Luca drawled before he picked up a kitten and nuzzled it.

"Are you sure you don't want another cat?" he asked Greer.

Greer looked between her men who shrugged.

Ford cleared his throat. "We have the space. And right now, we're outnumbering the cat. Might as well add some more."

Greer beamed and Luca looked ten feet taller.

"Oh good. We'll get these babies checked out, and then either you choose the ones you want, or the ones that connect to the other resident of the house."

"Oh, I'm so excited," Greer said.

We kept talking cats and cheese as we went over to the dining area where the food and drinks were spread out.

I tapped August's shoulder and pulled him back. "You okay? Do you want to talk about it?" I asked.

August shook his head. "No, I'm fine. Just weird as always. I like being here with her though. I like that we're a big family. I just hate sometimes the memories hit hard, you know?"

I nodded and rubbed my chest.

"Yeah. Well, we're okay. Right?"

"Always." He narrowed his gaze. "Except for the fact that you didn't tell me that my ex-wife lives here."

Everybody paused. Greer's eyes went wide as I turned to look at him.

"How the hell did you find out?"

August smiled, though it didn't look happy. I still didn't know why they had broken up. Why everything had fizzled, and while I wanted to ask, I knew it wasn't the time to do so. Though, when the hell would it be?

"One of my coworkers was in the bar and overheard you. And decided to run to tell me." He rolled his eyes. "She's a menace, not my ex, the coworker. She loves gossip, and wanted to make sure that I knew what was going on so I wouldn't be surprised." He rolled his eyes again. "But she did it in that southern drawl and spoke really slowly, as if waiting for a reaction."

I winced and rocked back on my heels. "Fuck. I wasn't sure how to tell you."

"Are you okay?" Greer asked.

August nodded. "I'm fine. I don't hate Paisley. I promise. We just aren't together anymore. I knew she had some family connection out here, but I didn't realize she had moved. I should have. Because we had been friends. But it's fine. I'm fine. I just, you know, probably should have known. And I don't hate you for not telling me," he said quickly. "Hell, how were you supposed to bring it up?"

"I was honestly thinking about it tonight. Though I didn't know how to start that conversation."

"And she is your girlfriend's boss."

Greer's eyes widened as she looked between us. "This is so much information right now. Seriously, girlfriend? Paisley? I need the details."

"Well, Paisley's my ex-wife. As you know. But she lives here now, and owns a large company that has a matchmaking section, and organizes small businesses. I don't really know what it all does, but her head of PR is Devney. Our brother's girlfriend."

Noah and Ford looked between us, smiles on their faces as they just sat back and listened to us volley back and forth. Luca bounced on his heels, interested as Greer clapped her hands.

"Devney? I love her. She's so sweet. And I honestly didn't realize who she worked for." She looked at August. "I would've told you." Then she winced and looked at me. "Not that I'm saying you should have. Wow, this is awkward."

I laughed, letting the awkwardness settle in. "Hell. It's family. It's supposed to be awkward."

Luca smiled. "That sounds like our motto."

"Our motto is more cult-like, so I like yours better,"

Noah put in, as Ford laughed into his beer and Greer glared at both of them.

"Shush. I'm learning all these new things, and I need to know what your intentions for Devney are," she said, hands on her hips.

I leaned forward and tapped her on the nose. "None of your business, little sister."

"Excuse me? You three showed up and demanded to know what these two's intentions were with me. I'm not quite sure you have a leg to stand on."

"You know, that's true," Luca put in.

"So, tell us about Devney."

I just shook my head. "We're friends."

"The way you two look at each other looks like more than friends."

I sipped my water, delaying my response. "We're just getting to know one another. I don't think we've put labels on anything yet."

"Well, I know that I was invited to a family dinner that was a big thing, but I didn't feel ready, so you should bring Devney. We can make it a tradition. To embarrass our family members, but not embarrass the ones they bring over." She beamed as she said it, and my heart grew, knowing that this was what she wanted, and I would do anything for her. Just like I would do anything for Devney.

When had life gotten so complicated?

"Yeah, I guess we can make it a thing."

August whistled under his breath.

"And Devney will be the canary in the Cassidy coal mine. I like it."

"Now, who are you dating?" I asked Luca, but Luca gestured towards the sound of kittens on the other side of the room.

"Does it really look like I have time to date?" And then I wanted to curse myself, as I remembered why Luca didn't date, and it had nothing to do with the kittens in the next room. But thankfully, August picked up the ball and started to ask about the wedding, and we sat down to eat, laughing and enjoying each other's company.

I sat back and breathed it all in.

We weren't perfect. We were still figuring things out. But we were getting better.

And while I might have accidentally offered to throw Devney to the wolves. I knew she could handle it.

Though I didn't know what I wanted her to handle.

Chapter Eight

Devney

"Yes, we can totally do that. Don't worry. You've got this. You're a pro at this. Don't worry. You've done this before, and we will keep doing it. Right. Right. You've got it."

As I hung up, I sighed and pinched the bridge of my nose.

"So, I hear they got it?"

I jumped and looked up at Paisley, who stood in my doorway, grinning at me.

I rolled my eyes and set down my phone. "I love our clients. Truly. Even when they make me want to pull my hair out. But seriously, this woman."

I just shook my head, and Paisley laughed.

"I know. She calls every day and asks the same questions, and you always have answers for her. And you're always polite. And you're right, she does have it. She can do it. And she's been doing it."

"I just feel really bad. I should know how to make things easier for her, and I don't really think I can."

Paisley came forward and took a seat in front of me, crossing her long, lean legs. Today she wore a coal gray pencil skirt with a bright pink top that had a tie on the front, as well as shoes to match the top. She looked like a Barbie with red hair, and it somehow all worked. I felt dumpy in comparison with my heather gray pants and mint green shirt with my blond hair up in a partial braid.

My shoes were kicked off underneath my desk, and I thought about trying to reach for them, but I didn't care. I knew Paisley did the same thing. We didn't have to wear heels at this job. We could pretty much wear whatever we wanted as long as we still looked presentable to our clients, but I liked wearing heels. And I also liked not wearing them.

"I am forever grateful that I hired you."

I smiled. "Really?"

"Yes, really. You're amazing at what you do. You keep our clients at ease, and they never feel like they're interrupting or in the way. You've got a way about you."

I shook my head. "It doesn't feel like it sometimes. But I'm so glad you see it that way. Considering it's what I'm trying to do."

"You're head of PR, and you kick ass at it. I'm grateful that you're with me and not some other company."

"What other company would I be at? This place is great. You not only have a subsidiary of venture capital that you work on, but you help smaller businesses that need to expand. You keep food in people's mouths. And, of course, there's the matchmaking thing."

Paisley rolled her eyes.

"You make me sound altruistic. When in essence, I'm spending money to make money. I sound like a finance bro."

I snorted and shook my head. "My best friend is a finance bro. She calls herself that because she has to deal with the real finance bros every day."

Paisley shuddered. "No, thank you. As soon as I was able, I opened my own business. I still put the blood sweat and tears into it to make sure it's *my* business. I have to go to meetings and galas and other events with those business bros, but I don't have to answer to them every day."

I shook my head and sat back, reaching for my coffee. I got an iced coffee today, and it hit the spot. "I'm not sure how Addison deals with it. Seriously. She loves her job, but she also has to deal with those finance bros who think that she's just their secretary. They even asked her to get coffee yesterday—at her own meeting where she was showing the financials and was presenting her case. It's ridiculous."

My stomach still twisted for Addison over that. Remembering how angry she was when she paced my living room, calling the men she worked with all sorts of names.

"You would think in this day and age there would at least be a little more progress."

"It's very much the 'Boys' Club' there, even though Addison isn't the only woman."

"And somehow our business is the opposite. Sometimes I feel like I need to add more dude-bros for flair."

We both shuddered at that.

"No, the men who work here treat women with respect and dignity. It's shocking."

"I know, right? Completely shocking."

"Anyway, I didn't come here just to complain about men, because I don't actually do that all the time."

I sat back in my chair, finishing my coffee.

"Same. I'm sorry about that."

"Anyway, I also wanted to apologize for the thing that we both have been really good about not talking about for the past couple of weeks."

I set my empty cup on my desk. "It's okay. We really don't have to talk about it."

Paisley gave me a look. "No, I think we really do. I'm sorry. For beginning our conversation by lamenting that I had been stood up on my blind date."

"I'm still angry about that. Who the hell would stand you up?"

"The last guy that I'll ever use a dating app for. It's fine, I don't need a date. I'm perfectly fine just running this business and making friends. Not that I have a lot of friends because I'm busy. But well, you know, I'm trying."

She smiled so brightly that we both knew it was fake. And I knew right then and there I was going to have to change that. I had been working for Paisley for over a year now, and I loved my job. And I liked Paisley. She worked hard, and if we were doing something wrong, she sat us down and made sure we knew how to do it right rather than yelling at us like my first boss. She also praised us when we were doing things right, and we were paid a fair wage. It was a good place. I was friends with a lot of my coworkers. We got along, and we also had our boundaries.

But I realized that we really didn't get to know Paisley that well. She was an island. And we were just surrounding her, trying to catch up.

"You've never asked about August." She paused again. "Have you met him yet?" she asked softly, and I couldn't read her voice. Maybe I was thinking too hard about it...or maybe I needed to know more. Paisley was becoming my friend and I knew this subject was delicate.

"I haven't yet. Mostly because, well, Heath and I are taking things slow, I guess. And between our jobs, we don't see each other too often? Okay maybe often, but not daily. We haven't done the family thing yet. I don't know when or if we will because I don't know if I'm ready for that."

She smiled at me, and again I couldn't read her. What had gone on between her and August? It wasn't my place to ask. But I wanted to know. I wanted to know who had hurt who, and how sticky it would get for what was about to come.

"The Cassidys are really great. I didn't get to know the sister. Greer. August and I weren't married long enough, and they weren't close enough for that to happen. But the brothers? They're a unit. It's nice. Even when they don't think they're close, that they can't rely on each other, they can. Heath's a good man, from what I remember. And while fate is being a bitch by throwing my past back in my face, I'm glad you're seeing him." She paused, looked at me. "You *are* seeing him, right? And I'm not just making this even more awkward by bringing up a past situation?"

I laughed, I couldn't help it. "Yes, we're still seeing each other. Like I said, just slowly."

"How slow are we talking?" Then Paisley held up both her hands. "You know, we're on the clock. And I shouldn't ask such inappropriate questions when I'm your boss."

"We are on the clock, and I know you have a meeting

coming up. So how about we go out for a drink tonight?" I held up my hands. "Not at Heath's bar."

"You know what," she said after a moment, staring at me with an odd intensity. I wished I could read her face. "That sounds good. I'd love to. Like I said, after I moved out here from Portland, I didn't make a lot of friends. I was ambitious with my job, and I wanted this company to do great. So I made a lot of contacts, but no one I could go out and be comfortable with."

"You're going to regret saying that. I'm not a clinger, but I never let go of my friends. I mean, Addison left me for a bit so she could finish school at this top-notch program, and we had to do the long-distance friendship thing, which sucked. But now she's back, and she's my best friend, and the three of us are having a drink tonight. Just warning you."

"Are you sure? I don't want to impose."

"Addison doesn't even know she's coming tonight. I just invited her. So don't worry, you guys are all mine. I promise. You're going to love her."

"She seemed nice for the two seconds that I got to meet her."

I laughed right as my phone rang.

"Okay, 7:00 p.m. tonight? Is that too late?"

"No, that's good, since we have that late meeting."

"True. We won't be out too late either. How about at P Six's?"

"Perfect." Paisley stood up. "Thank you. For being kind. And not asking too many questions."

"You know I can't promise anything after I've had a few drinks. I'm just saying. I probably can't promise anything after I've had a sip."

She laughed and shook her head. "Same. But I'll try to restrain myself. I liked Heath. He was a good guy. And I like you, Devney. So, just have fun. And I'd say be careful, but that would sound ominous."

She smiled and headed out of my office, and once again I wondered what had happened. But I knew it wasn't my place to ask. Not until she was ready to tell me.

P Six was a rooftop bar in downtown Denver that had a gorgeous bohemian look to it. Half of the bar was indoors while the other half was outdoors, and it truly depended on the weather gods if where you sat was good. Tonight though, it was comfortably warm, not too cool, not too breezy. And there wasn't snow or ice on the ground, considering it could snow in June in Denver, depending on those weather gods. They had the portable heaters turned on though; as soon as the sun went down, the temperature dropped, but it was still gorgeous out. I loved this place, and because it was a weeknight, it wasn't too busy. I didn't usually go out to bars with friends on a weeknight, but tonight was needed.

"I really don't have time for this, but I'm so happy that you asked me here," Addison said, and I smiled at my friend.

"Of course, you're with me till the end of the line," I said with a wink.

"It has been the week from hell at work, and I really can't talk about it because half of it's covered by an NDA, but let's just say I needed this."

"So did I," I said as I reached forward and squeezed her hand. "Paisley should be here any minute. Her meeting was a bit longer than mine, and she told me to go on ahead."

"I'm excited to get to know your boss. She doesn't seem like a completely evil person."

I laughed. "She's not. She's pretty cool. Even though I'm still getting to know her."

"And she's okay with you dating Heath? Considering he's the twin of her ex-husband."

"There's a story there, but it's not ours to know yet."

"I'm just glad that we're all getting out."

"Even though *somebody's* been going out more recently," Addison said as Paisley walked up.

"Yes, I'd love to know all about that," she said with a wink as she took a seat on one of the lower couch areas with us.

The waiter, one we had been trying to get the attention of the entire time, barreled over as soon as Paisley sat down, and Addison and I looked at each other before we burst out laughing.

Paisley frowned for a minute, and I held up my finger motioning that I would tell her in a moment.

We ordered different martinis, as well as bottles of water, and then we sat back, Addison and I still giggling.

"What?" Paisley asked.

"We've been here for a good ten minutes and we couldn't get his attention, but as soon as you showed up with those long legs and gorgeous red hair, he was ready."

Paisley rolled her eyes. "Maybe it was just timing. You guys are gorgeous. I mean seriously, it's not the legs."

"Maybe it's the hair," Addison said. "I love it."

Paisley slid her hands through her hair and smiled. "I had a Brazilian blowout a while ago, and it's starting to wear off, so the frizziness is coming back, which is saying something because Denver doesn't give you frizz."

"My hair's slightly wavy but goes full curl as soon as I hit anywhere humid."

"I do not have that problem no matter where I go. I straighten mine no matter what." Addison grinned, and then leaned back as the drinks came. We took ours and clinked them together.

"To new beginnings," I said, and they both nodded.

"To new beginnings," they said in unison.

I sipped my drink, happy that I ordered a straight-up Grey Goose martini, because I could sip it slow and not need another one. If I got anything too sweet, I downed those a little too quickly, and it was a work night.

"Thank you for this. Seriously. I think I need a little more time away from the office."

"Ditto," Addison said as she gestured her drink towards Paisley.

"I would say that too, but you are my boss," I said with a roll of my eyes.

"Well, I am demanding. I know it, and it bothers most people."

"Honestly, it doesn't bother me. And I'm not just trying to kiss your ass here."

"True, and so we don't cross any lines you're not comfortable with, we don't have to talk about work at all. Unless you want to, Addison."

Addison shook her head at Paisley's words. "No, let's not. All I do is talk about work. I know what we *could* talk about though," Addison said with a flutter of her eyelashes.

I sipped my water. "Oh no, let's talk about the weather. It's been gorgeous, hasn't it?"

"Tell us all about Heath. So have you, you know," Addison put in, and I blushed harder.

"I take it that's a no. Really?" Paisley added.

"Not yet. We're taking it slow." I cleared my throat.

"I'm a virgin. And he's taking it really slow. Even though I feel like I'm dying inside."

"Oh. Really. I'd say good for you, unless...is that what you want me to say? Sorry, I'm really not good at girl talk."

I waved her off. "It wasn't on purpose, it just sort of happened. Between school and work and life, it just never happened. And Heath is going super slow and being really kind, but I know that he has a life outside of me and outside of what I want. We both just said this is a good time. I'm not going to feel too much about it, and I'm going to have a fling." I paused. "I've never had a fling before. But I guess you need to be flung first?"

Both Paisley and Addison burst out laughing.

"Yes, getting flung would be nice. And when that happens, you're going to have to give us all of the details," Addison said, still giggling.

"Though maybe you want to keep it to yourself, but you don't have to hide any details from me, considering I was married to his twin."

I looked at Paisley, before I shook my head. "Okay, this isn't going to be awkward at all," I said sarcastically.

"Oh, I'm having a blast."

"There is another brother you know," I teased, and Addison's eyes widened.

"You know what? I'm okay. Really okay. I have enough of men at work. Seriously though, just live and be. Enjoy yourself. When it happens, it happens. Take care of yourself, and from what I've seen of Heath, he'll take care of you."

Addison cleared her throat. "And don't throw yourself into labels too quickly, try not to get hurt. It's okay if you just figure out what you want."

I sipped my drink and sat back as we talked about celebrities we found attractive, and the latest movies none of us had seen.

I didn't know what I wanted with Heath. Mostly because I hadn't let myself think about it. It had been a few weeks since we met for real, but we hadn't slept together.

I wanted that. I was just afraid to want more.

When we finished our drinks and left, I had also finished a full bottle of water, so was ready to drive home. I was tired, but a good tired. I'd had a good day.

I had been ignoring my phone for most of the evening, and my family was on a text roll.

The sibling group chat with all eleven of us was blowing up, and since it wasn't after nine yet, I answered.

Me: I love you all, I was just out with friends. Stop worrying about me.

Every single text consisted of asking where I was and why I wasn't answering and if they needed to call the National Guard. And knowing my siblings, they would do it.

Maureen: You should have answered us. We were worried.

Me: You're not my parents. I'm fine. Promise.

Elizabeth: Were you out with Heath?

Me: No, but it wouldn't be your business even if I was. Seriously, I'm fine. Go to bed. Hug your family.

They kept going and I ignored them, muting the chat. They knew I was alive, and now that I was home, I could ignore them for longer.

Then my phone beeped again, and I wondered if someone had slid through the muting. But it was Heath.

My stomach did that twisting thing; I told myself to ignore it, because this was only just for fun. He was just being kind and was just a good guy. I didn't want to ask too much too quickly.

Heath: I have to close tonight, so I don't know if I'm going to be able to have our phone call like I like. But I hope you had a fun time tonight. Date tomorrow?

I bit my lip, telling myself that this was just a fling.

Only it didn't feel like a fling.

And that was a problem.

Me: I just got home from drinks with the girls. I have a few work things to do and then I'm going to bed. But tomorrow would be nice.

Heath: Sleep well. Don't work too hard.

I set down my phone and put my hand on my stomach.

I was ready. It was about time. All I wanted was Heath. Even though it might be too much for me. Even though I might be too much for him.

But I could have this.

As long as I didn't get ahead of myself.

Chapter Nine

Heath

Another hike, and another moment where I felt I was bursting at the seams with want for her, but no matter what, I was going to control myself and not push.

At least I hoped so.

"I feel like I'm cheating on my bar," I said after a minute, and Devney grinned up at me.

"It sure feels like that, doesn't it?"

We followed the hostess towards the booth in the back.

"It's okay, I promise I won't tell your bar," she said with a laugh. I followed her, doing my best to take in the atmosphere of the bar, rather than watching her ass like I wanted to.

It was getting harder and harder to focus when she

was around because I wanted her. And not just for that sweet ass. But because of her smile, the way she made me laugh, and the way she just made things feel *right*. That was going to be a problem later, but I ignored it. There were other things on my mind, like the fact that my brothers and her best friend were meeting us on this date of ours.

"Addison's going to be outnumbered with us, you think she's really going to be okay?" I asked as we took a seat in the large horseshoe-shaped booth. I sat at the edge and she sat next to me.

She smiled. "She can handle her own. Believe me, with her job? She can handle you Cassidy brothers far easier than you think."

"Honestly, I don't doubt that. She's scary, but in a good way."

"That's what I like to hear," Addison said from behind.

I grinned at her. "I knew you were there," I lied. I got out of the booth and gestured for her to take a seat. Devney got out and hugged her best friend.

"I'm so happy that you're here. I was afraid that you would have to work late."

Addison winced. "Honestly, me too. It's been a tough few weeks, but I'm making do. Somewhat. I made it work. I promised I would. Plus, I could use time away."

I didn't know what was going on with Devney's

friend, but I loved the way the two seemed to always be there for each other. While Devney's family was a little overwhelming, and never really let her out of their sight, her friend seemed to care, but not in an overbearing way. I knew that her siblings had already texted her a few more times, just to see what she was doing tonight, and if I was still treating her right. They didn't tell her what to do in the text, but they wanted to make sure she was safe.

While it grated on me, maybe I was wrong to be annoyed by it. Maybe I just didn't know how other people acted. Or how siblings were supposed to act. After all, we were still learning what the hell we were doing as a family.

"So, have you guys ordered anything to drink?" Addison asked, and I shook my head.

"We beat you by ten seconds, if that. So don't worry."

"Do we want to open a bottle?" Devney asked, looking at the menu. "Though I don't know if your brothers like wine."

"They like pretty much anything."

"What do we like?" Luca asked, a bright grin on his face. He must have had a good day, and I was glad. Luca didn't smile much anymore. I knew why, our family knew why, but I hadn't told Devney yet. It wasn't my place.

"I said that you'll drink anything. We were thinking about getting a bottle of wine."

August nodded. "Sounds good. That and some sparkling water? I've been on a sparkling water kick."

"Considering you drank the entire case that I brought over for myself, yes, you are," Luca said with a roll of his eyes. "And hi. I'm Luca. This is August, he looks just like that other one. Therefore, I'm the prettiest."

"I'm not sure that works that way," I said dryly.

"Yeah, I'm the pretty one," August replied.

"You know, I am going to have to disagree," Devney said with a wink, and I put my arm around her shoulders.

"See? My girl says I'm the prettiest."

"Oh, how cute, adorable, I can barely breathe through the beauty of it," Luca said as he rolled his eyes. Then he looked at Addison. "You must be Addison."

"I am. And you must be the one who's trying to foist off kittens?"

"Do you need a kitten? I have a few. They're loving, therefore you'd always have a friend at home." He paused. "Unless you'd like me to be your friend at home," he added, and Addison threw her head back and laughed.

"Is that really the line you went with?" August asked as he pushed Luca out of the way and took the seat next to Addison. Luca scooted in on the other side of him, and then we were all talking and laughing, and ended up ordering a bottle of wine, and then a second. Between the five of us, it didn't amount to too many glasses, and we did order the sparkling water.

"No, seriously, you cannot tell me he is the best Superman. I'm sorry. There's just no way."

Luca glared at Addison. "Yes, he is. He is the best. The way that he personifies the character, the way that he brought through the connection of right versus wrong."

"Did you not remember the CGI messing with his mouth? They could have just shaved his face. Or not done the re-shoots at all. It's ridiculous."

"Okay, you've got me there," Luca said with a wince. "He's still the best."

"And Superman murdered someone. A lot of some-ones, if you include the fact that he knocked down all those buildings."

"And, what, Batman's all good?"

"Do not get me started on the best Batman. Michael Keaton will always be the best."

"Didn't that movie come out before you were born?" Devney asked, and Addison waved her off.

"So? That doesn't mean he wasn't the best."

"Do you have any idea what they're talking about?" August asked, and I shook my head.

"Sadly no."

Addison's eyes widened. "You don't know who Michael Keaton is?" she asked, her voice high-pitched.

"I know who he is. I just don't have any thoughts on my favorite Superman or Batman. I'm a Marvel guy."

Carrie Ann Ryan

"Okay, Captain America or Iron Man?" she asked, and I sighed.

"If I say the wrong answer, are you going to forbid me from seeing Devney?"

"Honestly, maybe."

"It's okay, I can make my own choice. If I can fight the sibs in order to have a life, I can probably fight her. Maybe."

Luca just sighed. "You like Iron Man, don't you."

"Of course, I do. He's fighting for the wrongs that he made."

"Yet it isn't so cut and dry. He doesn't truly atone for the mistakes he made, he just puts them on the other people around him."

They continued to fight, though it sounded more playful than anything. I didn't know if there was a connection there, beyond just friends. I wasn't sure I could deal with Devney's best friend and my brother dating, but it didn't seem that was what was happening. If anything, it felt like she clicked with us. Which was good because I wanted to spend more time with Devney. It had been a while since I'd been in a relationship, and this *was* a relationship, even if we were figuring out what we wanted.

"Do we want dessert?" August asked, leaning back in his seat. "I'm still hungry."

124

"You ate an entire steak, and part of Devney's. How could you still be hungry?"

August shrugged. "I was grading papers over lunch and skipped it by accident."

"Oh, we can order you something else. Don't worry," Devney said, and I frowned.

"Don't be nice to him. He stole your food."

"I wasn't going to finish mine anyway, because I ate tons of bread. I love bread."

"Bread is life," Luca replied.

"Damn straight," Devney agreed.

"Still though. Don't be nice to him."

"Because he's your twin, or because he took the last bite of my steak before you could?"

"She's got you there," Luca said with a grin.

"I like you guys, you all joke around, but you're not constantly trying to outdo one another."

"You clearly haven't seen us on Thanksgiving playing football."

I sighed at Luca's words. "Seriously. We're not great at it."

"Not great at football? Or not great at stopping fighting?" Devney asked.

"Both," August said with a laugh, and I flipped him off.

"I'm way better than you."

"You wish."

"I feel like at any moment they're going to start beating their chests and playing football in the middle of this restaurant," Addison said dryly.

"Maybe, but I'd like the show," Devney answered.

I leaned forward and pressed a quick kiss to her lips. "Maybe later."

"Was that a turn-on?" Luca asked. "I'm not used to my big brother flirting like this. It's nice. Good job, Devney."

She blushed, and I narrowed my eyes at Luca. "Be nice."

"I am being nice. I like Devney. I have said that behind your back, and it is nice to also say it to your face. You're kind of cool."

"Well, I try. Actually, I don't try," she corrected. "I'm not good at that whole thing."

"You do pretty good," I whispered.

"Okay, let's talk about your favorite Star Wars movie," Addison said, to change the subject.

"Dangerous ground," August said, and I nodded, knowing that if we weren't careful, Luca and Addison were probably going to get in a fight over dessert.

By the time we finished, I was full and my sides ached from laughing.

It didn't even feel like we were fifth-wheeling anybody. Devney and Addison just fit in with us.

"I'm sorry Greer couldn't come."

"She's on a camping trip with the guys, so she said she was sorry. But next time."

Devney looked up at me, eyes darkening. "I'd like that. A next time."

I leaned down and pressed my lips to hers.

"Next time works."

"Heath?" she asked, her voice soft.

I swallowed. "Yes?"

"Take me home?" she asked, before kissing me again.

Because it was about time, and I couldn't hold back any longer.

I wasn't sure I wanted to.

I didn't remember the drive back to her place. I knew I drove the speed limit because getting pulled over with my cock so hard it was ready to burst probably wasn't the best. We somehow made it, somehow got out of the car, and didn't fall on top of each other as soon as we got inside. Instead, we stood in her living room, my hands in her hair, my mouth over hers as she raked her fingernails down my back.

"We can go slow. I swear. We don't have to do this right now."

"I swear to God, Heath. If you do not fuck me right now, you're going to watch me finger myself. Like I said, I know how to get off. Just because I haven't used a man to do it, doesn't mean I don't know how to get it done."

"Fuck," I growled, before I bent down and tossed her over my shoulder.

She let out a grunt of surprise as I smacked her ass and carried her down the hallway. I looked in one room, realized it was an office, then another that had to be a guest room. Finally, I found the master bedroom, stomped inside, and tossed her on the bed. She bounced a bit, her legs kicking in the air as she laughed.

"Well then, going all caveman?"

"Let's get your pants off and see exactly how caveman I can get."

"What are you going to do, bang me with your club?" she asked, and I burst out laughing.

"How many sex puns do you have waiting for this?"

"I'm very nervous, so I have a whole list of sex puns. It's quite long."

I rolled my eyes, before I pulled at her ankle.

She let out a squeal as I kissed her ankle over her jeans, and then worked on her boots.

"I wish these were sandals and you could just kick them off. Instead you have double knots on these fucking things."

"I'd say we could keep them on and just shuck my jeans down, but I'm not sure that's the sexiest thing in the world."

The image of her on her hands and knees with my cock in her mouth and her shoes still on nearly sent me over the edge and I groaned.

"Oh, maybe another time."

"Now I want to know what you're thinking."

When I told her, she sat up and groaned, tugging at my pants.

"Let's get these off," she said.

Somehow, I got her shoes off, and then I was kissing her again, hovering over her.

I tossed my shirt over my head, and when she sucked in a breath, I grinned.

"Whoa," she whispered.

"That's sweet, very sweet."

This was only supposed to be fun. I liked her, I wanted to get to know her, and I liked the way she squirmed. But now I really wanted to make her squirm. We kissed some more, and when I pulled off her shirt, she groaned when I leaned down and cupped the lace covering her breasts.

"Beautiful," I whispered, before I kissed between her breasts, and then down her stomach. I undid her jeans and pulled them down over her legs. "So beautiful, baby. Are you sure?"

"Yes. I promise. You don't have to keep asking."

I looked up at her and frowned.

"It's your first time. But it's also *our* first time. So, of course, I'm going to ask you exactly what you want, and how you want it. I may think I know how to get you off, and how to make it feel good, but I still want to double-check. Let's make sure. Let's make this right."

She looked up at me, and I was afraid I'd said the wrong thing, but she swallowed hard and slid her hands through my hair.

"Okay," she whispered. I leaned down and kissed over her belly button. She wore a tiny lace thong and seeing that made me groan.

"You wore this hiking?"

"I know, I know, but it was either that or nothing."

"Damn you, woman." I leaned down further to kiss over her pussy and she bucked off the bed. I pressed my hands to her hips.

"I'll take it slow."

"Maybe not too slow," she whispered.

But I just smiled and tugged her panties to the side.

She was already wet, soft and glistening in pretty pink. When I licked, she groaned, shaking.

"Heath."

"I want to make sure you're ready."

"From what I already feel, I know I'm ready."

"Let's just double-check. I don't want you to hurt."

"You can't hurt me, Heath."

She sounded so sincere, but I wasn't sure. But I could

make tonight good enough. I could make it what she needed.

I licked and I sucked at her, tasting her sweet honey over my tongue. When I slid my thumb over her clit, she bowed off the bed as she came.

"Heath!"

I smiled against her pussy as I continued to eat her out, sucking and licking. I slowly inserted one finger inside her and she clenched around me, tight.

Too tight.

Fuck. I had never been with a virgin before. I had never been with someone without experience. But I would make tonight perfect for her. No matter how slow we had to go. I might burst in my own jeans, but it would be worth it.

I worked my finger in and out of her, stretching her sweet folds. She groaned against me, her hips rocking on my hand. I gently inserted a second finger and she let out a slight wince. I froze.

"Are you okay, baby?"

"It just feels so big."

I smiled against her thigh.

"We just need to get you ready for my cock."

Her eyes widened and she undid her own bra. I reached up and cupped her breasts, her sweet light pink nipples pebbling underneath my palm. She was so fucking beautiful. It was hard for me to think.

I continued to work her, soft and slow, kissing up and down her body, my hand between her legs.

When she finally came again, clenching around my finger, I let her come down slowly.

"We can stop here," I whispered against her lips. "We don't have to go further than this."

She tugged on my hair and glared at me.

"I want this, Heath. As long as you do, I want this."

I pressed my forehead against hers, my breath choppy. "Damn straight. I want you, Devney. I've wanted you since the first time I saw you."

She blinked and a few tears escaped. I kissed them away before taking her lips again. I slid my fingers along her entrance, before finally sitting up to undo my pants. I shucked them off, and her eyes widened at the sight of my dick.

"Are you okay?" I asked as I palmed myself, running my hand over the shaft and sliding my thumb along the tip. I was already way too close. I needed to breathe. Or this would go far quicker than she wanted.

"Okay," she said quickly. "I mean, I've watched porn, I know what penises look like. But I really wasn't expecting this."

I laughed, my shoulders shaking.

"You are seriously the perfect woman."

"You say the sweetest things. Now, please, may I touch your dick?" she asked.

I shook my head as I reached for her.

"You touch me, I'm going to come right away. And I want to make you feel good."

"You've already made me feel good. Twice."

"True, but it's still your turn."

"There're condoms in my side table. Just in case."

I smiled and kissed her softly. "I have some in my backpack. Just in case. I'll always keep you safe, Devney. I promise."

"Good. I trust you," she whispered, and I took her lips again before reaching for a condom. I slid it over my length and then settled between her thighs.

She tensed, her mouth parting, and I kept kissing her, bringing her closer to the edge again with my fingers and my mouth. And when she was wet, shaking, and ready, I slid between her legs again.

"Are you ready?" I asked, as I tangled my fingers with hers. She nodded, and I took her mouth before I slid inside as gently as I could. She groaned against me, but not from pain. Grateful, needy, and on edge, I worked my way into her until I was buried balls-deep, to the hilt. She wrapped her legs around my waist, and we both shook, the connection far too much.

I tried to be gentle, tried to take my time, but she smiled and moved with me thrust for thrust.

I moved at whatever rhythm she set. We panted and we groaned, and when she finally came, her mouth letting a sweet sigh escape, I followed her, taking her lips with my own, and rolling to the side so I didn't crush her when I collapsed.

My forehead pressed against hers, I held her close as she came down again, and smiled.

But inside, I screamed.

I was only supposed to be the good time. But I wanted more. More of this, more of *her*. I already knew I wanted more of her smiles.

I had no idea what she wanted.

I'd moved here to find myself again, to find my family. To find something more.

I was terrified I had just found it.

Now I had to figure out exactly what to do with that.

Chapter Ten

Heath

M **e:** Are you headed out tonight?

       Devney: If I can get through this meeting. We had a few emergencies.

Me: Okay. Just let me know if you need anything.

Not that I could actually help her with her job. I had no idea how to work in PR. But she was brilliant. And I loved seeing her work while sitting on my couch, typing away at things. I had been going through a few things for work too, but it felt different; I was just a bar owner. She was brilliant.

But I had to remember that I was supposed to be the initial fake date. The good time.

I wasn't allowed to want more.

Me: We are headed to dinner tonight, the guys and

me. Ace is coming too, since we are letting our staff close tonight.

Devney: Look at you, growing up and being the big boss.

Me: Yes, let's not talk about it, because it's kind of stressing me out.

I trusted our team. We had hired them, trained them, I knew they could handle it, but Ace and I loved our baby bar, and tended to work too many hours. But we were practicing giving more time to the rest of our staff because with the wedding coming up, we would be taking off for a few days.

We needed to make sure we were ready.

And not work sixty-hour weeks again.

Devney: We'll come see you later tonight, depending on our girls' night. Would it be weird if all of us showed up?

I knew what she was asking, and while I didn't care, I had to see if my brother would.

Me: I'm glad Paisley has you. I'll ask my brother if it's a problem. It shouldn't be but I don't want anyone to feel awkward.

Devney: It's just an odd coincidence and I don't want anyone to feel awkward, either. But we'll figure it out.

Me: Yeah, we will. I'm off. Don't work too hard.

Devney: I could say the same to you.

I smiled and ran my hand through my hair.

Then I picked up the phone and called my brother. August picked up on the first ring.

"Hey, am I running late? I thought I had an hour until we were meeting at your bar."

"No, I just have a question."

"Hit me."

I was silent for long enough, that August cursed under his breath.

"She's going to be there tonight, isn't she?"

I pinched the bridge of my nose. I was glad I hadn't done a video call. I loved my twin. But sometimes he could read my mind better than I could read his.

"She's Devney's boss. And they're becoming friends. I am sort of under the impression that when Paisley moved out here, she didn't have a lot of friends and was starting over. Like we are."

August cursed. "Damn it. Yeah, I can see that. She's really good at focusing on one thing and making sure it works. I'll get over it. Denver's a big city, but with you dating her friend, I can't really avoid her forever. It would be good to meet up at your place. It's sort of neutral ground, and sort of more my ground."

"I'm not going to ask you what happened, because you could tell me if you needed to."

"It's good that you understand that. There's no need to rehash it."

Carrie Ann Ryan

The problem was, I knew he was lying. They definitely needed to rehash it. But he was right, I *was* seeing Devney. And that wasn't going to change anytime soon, even though that thought surprised me.

"Anyway, I'll text Devney that she can bring the girls by during their barhopping tonight."

"Okay, Luca will like seeing Addison there."

"You think anything's going on there?"

"No, which is probably a good thing because Addison and Devney are best friends. But it's nice to see Luca smiling more and hanging out. Those two just clicked."

"Yeah. They did. It will be one big happy family."

"Since Greer's men are coming tonight, do you know if Greer's going with the girls?"

"Yep. And Ace's fiancée, Grace is going too. It's a big event."

"See? There's going to be so many people there it's not going to matter that my ex-wife is also there."

I was sure he wasn't telling the truth, but I just agreed and said my goodbyes.

I grabbed my things and headed to the bar. While I wasn't working today, I never really got a day off. I went in to make sure the team was ready to go.

"How are we doing?" I asked, and Ace looked up from the bar. I snorted and shook my head. "Look at us, the worst workaholics ever."

"Everything's fine, I was just helping out Denise."

"I didn't need any help, but I do appreciate you changing out the kegs."

"It's not that you can't lift them, it's that they're awkwardly wide. You can do it, but if I do it now, you can do the next ten later."

"Be still my beating heart. What would I do without a man helping me lift things?"

"Denise," I said with a roll of my eyes.

She waved me off. "I'm kidding. I appreciate you. And I really do hate the angle of that particular tap. It is a pain in the ass."

"You're right. I wonder if there's something we can do about it."

Ace studied it too and nodded. "Yeah, let's look into it."

"You guys don't have to fix something just because I said it was annoying."

"You're right, we don't, but if it's annoying you, and you actually said something about it, something you never do, that means it's probably annoying other people."

"That is true," she said with a laugh.

"So, we will work on it as a team."

Ace and I talked it over for a few minutes, and then my brothers, as well as Greer's men walked in.

I frowned and looked at the clock and realized more time had passed than I had thought.

"Damn it, we're running late."

"No worries, we assumed you'd be working," Luca said, and I looked at the contraption on his chest.

"Please don't tell me that is a dog in a baby carrier."

"It's not."

"It's a puppy," Noah said and laughed.

"Are you kidding me?"

"What? You don't have a no pets policy. You even have a lovely dog bowl outside in case it gets hot for the babies out there."

"I have a vet for a brother. Of course, this place is pet-friendly. Still, though, a baby carrier?"

A little furry head popped up from inside the carrier.

"What the hell is that?"

"Hey, be nice to your nephew."

"Really? You've adopted another baby?"

"Not exactly. He's just with me for another hour or two, until my team can come pick him up. But this is the only place he likes sleeping, because he likes the sound of a heartbeat. That's why we let him do it. Don't we, Pongo?"

"Pongo? That's its name?" I asked dryly.

"Pongo is very sweet, and loves us, doesn't he?"

Pongo licked Luca's chin. I just sighed before getting their drink orders.

"Boss, you're not working. Let me do this."

"I don't mind. You can work on the other group. We're going to be loud and obnoxious."

"Oh, that's just what I like to hear," she said with a laugh as she went over to Luca and rubbed the top of Pongo's head.

"You know, if I swung your way, the whole idea of a little puppy in a chest carrier would send me right over the edge."

"Well, you just let me know if you change your mind. I'll make sure to bring the cuteness."

"Oh you. You're adorable."

"She's talking to the dog, man," August said, and he flipped him off.

I grinned and set everyone's drinks in front of them. We were doing mostly beer tonight, and we had a few local brews that sounded interesting. I was trying a sour, because I was in the mood for it, and while it wasn't my usual, it sounded good because it was a hot day outside.

"When do you start on the huge science project?" Ace asked, and August cleared his throat.

"Next week. It's a month-long process for my AP class, and while it's my first one at this school, I've done it before."

"Are parents allowed to help?" I asked, sipping my beer.

"Yes, but not take over. I will be working late with office hours because some parents can't help. Either they don't remember the science, because who the hell is going to remember something from eleventh grade so long ago, or they just don't have time."

"See? That's why I like you. You think about the fact that not everybody can step in as much as other parents."

"And while we've already had some parent-teacher conferences where I've explained that while this project is going to happen a lot in class too, some of it does happen outside of class. I know these kids have sports and lives outside of school, so I'm trying to help while not being too much. You know?"

"You're a good guy, August."

As soon as I said the words, August's face closed down and he pressed his lips together. "Not in some people's minds," he mumbled, and I turned to see the girls walking in.

They were laughing at something, though I wasn't sure what, but they were all smiles, like they didn't have cares in the world. Even though I knew that they did, and today was going to be slightly awkward. But while I wanted to see Paisley's reaction to August and how my brother was going to handle it, I only had eyes for Devney.

She was gorgeous tonight, in a flowing peach-colored dress. She also wore these little wicker-looking wedges that had white straps, and she had painted her toes white.

She was so gorgeous, it was hard for me to breathe.

"You're here," Luca said as he pushed past me and went right up to Addison.

Addison ignored him and went straight for Pongo. She put out her hand, and Pongo sniffed it before putting his little paws up and reaching for her.

"Am I allowed to pick him up?"

"Go for it. But let's go sit over at the table so we don't annoy other people."

"Hello, Pongo. Luca told me all about you. Isn't this bar the best? Yes. But your Auntie Addison is here to make sure you have all of your daydreams and puppy dreams fulfilled." She held him like a baby as he sniffed her neck, and she took a seat on the other side of the booth from us.

"Hello, everyone," she said, but not looking at us. She only had eyes for Pongo.

"Well, we see where we stand," Devney said dryly as she came over. I put my arm around her waist and pulled her towards me, crushing my lips to hers.

Somebody wolf whistled, but I ignored them. I just wanted her taste.

"Hello," I whispered.

She looked up at me and licked her lips.

Oh yeah, this was it. Right here.

We had been together a few more times since that first time, but I still couldn't believe she was mine. For now.

"Hi," she breathed.

Greer rolled her eyes behind Devney when I finally looked up.

"Hello, your sister's here too," she said with a laugh.

"Sorry about that," I said, as I pulled Greer in for a hug, kissing the top of her head.

"Thanks for inviting me, I like being out like this," Greer said as she hugged me back. "Who knows, I might invite some of my friends, too, just take over the whole bar."

I shuddered as I looked over at Noah. "If you bring all of your family or Ford's, I'm going to have to open a second bar."

"Pretty much," Noah said with a laugh as he got up to hug my sister.

I ignored their deep kiss, and then her deep kiss with Ford. I didn't mind my baby sister being in love with two men. I did mind watching it.

"Get that look off your face," Devney said with a laugh. "You just made out with me in the middle of your bar, and you have a problem with that?"

I narrowed my gaze. "How the hell did you know what I was thinking?"

"Because you're scowling. It's pretty easy," she said.

I looked up, past Ace and Grace who were kissing sweetly, and over at Paisley. She stood awkwardly to the side before she cleared her throat.

"Hey, come on, let's get a drink."

I waved her off. "No, I'll go up and get it. I'm technically our server for the night."

Good Time Boyfriend

"I guess it pays to know the bartenders." Paisley grinned at me. "Thanks for letting me come. I've been enjoying hanging out with girls again."

"Hey, Paisley," Luca said from the table by Addison's side, the puppy bouncing between them.

"Hi, Luca." Then she turned to August, who stood on the other side of the table, beer in hand. "Hello, August. Good to see you again."

And for the life of me, I could not tell if that was a lie or not.

August smiled, then came around the booth, set his beer in front of Luca, and walked right up to Paisley. He held out his arms, and she rolled her eyes before she hugged him.

I met Devney's gaze, then Luca's, then my sister's, wondering what the hell was going on.

They hugged for a while, no words, before taking a step back.

"Good, glad that's over," Paisley said with a laugh while August just shook his head.

"Pretty much. Come on, you want your usual?"

"I could really use a beer."

August laughed and gestured towards the bar. "Pick what you want on tap. We'll get it for you. Since I'm his twin, I can pretend I work here, too."

"They can tell who you are," I called out.

"So you think," August said, and just like that, the tension dropped.

We ordered food, and Denise brought us the nachos and other items we ordered, and we laughed, drank, and got to know one another. And though August and Paisley sat on opposite sides of the table, there wasn't the tension I expected. Maybe it was because they were trying hard not to make it awkward, or maybe I really didn't know why they had gotten married and divorced in the first place.

I needed to know soon, because the curiosity was killing me, and from the look on Devney's face, it was killing her too.

When the girls went out to use the restroom all at once because, apparently, they did that no matter where they were, Ace grinned at me. "So, you and Devney huh? Getting serious?"

I choked on my beer, while Luca grinned. The puppy was long gone, his team member having come to pick Pongo up. Addison had pouted, but the puppy needed sleep, and I wasn't in the mood to have to clean up after it.

"Look at you, scaring our big brother," Luca said with a grin. Noah and Ford just sat back, sipping their beers. We had grilled them, so I guess this was only fair. They were enjoying it too much for my liking.

"We're just hanging out."

"Is that what they're calling it?" August asked dryly.

"Fine. We're enjoying each other's company. But she

hasn't had a boyfriend before, and I'm not good at relationships. So as soon as we put a fucking label on it, it's
going to get weird. So, let's just keep it as it is."

"Well, that makes sense," Ace said. "Are you taking
her to the wedding?"

"I haven't asked her yet."

August cursed under his breath as Greer's men
winced and Luca just shook his head.

"What?"

"Grace's been talking about the wedding all night, and
we're getting married in less than two weeks. Either you
go by yourself, which is fine because you're my best man
and you have to be there, or you let her know you want
her with you. But you should probably talk about it with
her."

"Fuck. We've just been busy, enjoying ourselves. I
didn't think about it. I wasn't trying to be an asshole."

"That just comes naturally," Luca teased.

I liked this side of my brother, the laughter, the joy.
But it also annoyed the fuck out of me.

I flipped him off as the girls came out of the bathroom,
Devney veering towards the bar. Well, it was now or
never.

I got up and the guys cheered me on. I ignored them,
as well as the looks of confusion from the women.

I walked up to Devney and put my hand on her hip.
She whirled, eyes wide, and I cursed.

"Sorry, it's me."

"Yeah, maybe don't do that when my back is turned and I'm at a bar."

"Sorry. Sorry, baby," I whispered before I pressed my lips to hers.

She smiled and I looked into her eyes. They weren't glassy, and she had only had one drink, so I figured it was a good time to ask.

"Hey, Ace's wedding is in a couple of weeks."

Devney grinned. "I know."

"Do you want to be my date?"

"Grace was wondering if you were going to ask me," she said dryly.

"Sorry," I said with a wince. "Between the bar and getting the wedding set up and all that crap, I hadn't really thought about it. Not that I don't think about you, it just, well, you know."

"I get it. You are his best man and have been getting ready for the wedding long before we started seeing each other. But yes, I would love to go to the wedding with you. It'll be nice to go to a wedding not for one of my numerous siblings."

That made me laugh. "Well, good. I already have their gift picked out from the registry, so you don't even have to worry about that. It'll be fun. I haven't taken a date to a wedding before."

"Me either, but I have a feeling my reason is different than yours."

"Well," I said, knowing that my cheeks were a little pink.

"Picking up wedding guests or bridesmaids seems to be the thing."

"Well, I am the best man, but the only person I'm picking up at this wedding will be you."

"Smooth."

"I try."

I leaned down and kissed her again. Denise cleared her throat, and we parted so we could order drinks for the table.

"So, Paisley and August?"

I held out a hand. "I have no fucking clue. Honestly."

"Also, I like that Addison and Luca seem to be getting along. I don't sense any chemistry, which is fine since she needs a friend, especially a guy who isn't an asshole."

"We're really going to have to roll up on her job and kick some asses, aren't we?" I asked as we picked up the trays of drinks.

"Maybe not. She can handle it herself. But I like that our groups are blending. And I hope there won't be any tension in the future with a certain couple."

"Your mouth to the Cassidy God's ears."

She laughed, and it was the greatest fucking sound in the world.

When we sat back down, she sat practically in my lap, since we were nearly out of space, and I just enjoyed the moment.

I had a date to a wedding.

And that meant I knew exactly who I'd be going home with.

And that was a pretty great fucking deal.

Chapter 11

Heath

I pulled at my tie, annoyed. "Why did I say I would wear this suit again?" I asked as Ace grinned at me.

"Because you're my best friend, my best man, and you don't have a choice."

"Fine, but I'm doing it for Grace. Not you."

"I'm fine with that. Now, how do I look?"

Ace held out his arms and I took a good look at him in his perfectly tailored gray suit. Ace had trimmed his beard a little, but it was still long enough to reach his chest if he bent his head just right. He had conditioned it within an inch of its life, and it looked shiny and perfect. He had also actually brushed his hair, so it didn't look like he'd been running his hands through it all day. Though I knew that would change once he got nervous and was saying his vows. But that's how his fiancée liked it.

"My baby boy's growing up. One day you're learning how to pour a Guinness, the next day you're marrying an accountant."

Ace flipped me off. "I can't help it, I love her. And look at you, bringing your girlfriend to this rather than hooking up with some bridesmaid. Please don't hook up with the bridesmaid. It's Grace's sister, and she's married, and then I'd have to kick your ass, not just for destroying a marriage, but for hurting Devney. It'd be a whole thing."

I frowned. "You really think I'd do that? Not just to her sister, but to Devney? Is that what kind of guy you think I am?"

"Fuck, no. Sorry. I'm just rambling because I'm nervous. I'm about to say the vows that I've wanted to say for years to the woman that I love. We were bachelors forever, Heath. I've seen shit, lived through shit. Just like you have. I never wanted to be tied down. That wasn't what I thought my purpose would be.

"But now she's here, and I don't want to be with anyone else. I can't see myself being with anyone else. I want to proclaim to all of our friends and family and the rest of the fucking world that she's mine. And I'm hers. That's the thing. It's not ownership, it's a branding of each other. I want the world to know that we're each other's, and we don't fucking care what anyone else thinks."

For some reason I choked up. "Practicing your vows on me?"

"I'd tell you to fuck off, but then you might just leave and not give me away."

I laughed. "I don't think that's what a best man does."

"Maybe they should. Maybe we should have had August be our flower girl. Skipping down the aisle throwing rose petals."

"Don't say that to him, or he'll find a fanny pack of rose petals."

"Oh my God, please let me find a fanny pack for him. I'm sure Grace would love it."

"The next wedding, we'll make that happen."

"Your wedding?" Ace asked, and while I knew he was teasing, my throat closed up again.

"We're just seeing each other. Just taking it slow. Hell, she's never had a serious relationship before."

"You're allowed to want more. You're allowed to see yourself as more. You're not your parents, you know."

"Really? You're going to bring up *my* parents on your wedding day? It feels like bad luck."

"I shouldn't have, sorry. But seriously, she's good for you."

"I know she's good for me. You don't need to tell me that."

"Okay, I won't. Unless you do something stupid."

"That's not giving me much hope. You know I'm going to do something stupid. It's what we do."

"Your sister's not doing anything stupid."

I snorted. "Well, true, but for all I know, she's just waiting to do the stupid thing until later."

"You don't actually believe that, do you?"

I paced, annoyed with myself for even bringing it up. Because no, I wasn't sure I even believed it. But that didn't mean I needed to bring it up now. My parents were proof positive that even if you believed in getting married, if you believed you loved someone, you weren't always sure. You were most likely going to fuck something up and hurt people. And I didn't want to be that person. It wasn't in me. It wasn't in me to walk the same path they had. But I wasn't going to think about that right now. It was all I could do just to make sure that I didn't fuck up what I had with Devney before it was too late. So, I would do my best not to do that, and I would wait for her to walk away, so I wouldn't screw everything up.

But I wasn't quite sure I knew what I was doing on that note either.

"Come on, let's get you married. We don't need to worry about my future or my parents. They have nothing to do with this."

"Heath," Ace began, but I shook my head.

"Seriously. We're good. Go get married. Go have a life that has nothing to do with whatever promises my parents make to each other."

Ace frowned as his father came in and told us we

needed to be at the front of the area so my best friend could get married.

And I would try not to be a little cloud of doom.

And probably fail.

But I had to have hope. Hell, I had hope for my sister, didn't I? And Ace.

I just didn't need any hope for myself. Not today, not tomorrow.

Not when Devney deserved so much better.

I was just her first, that was all.

And it would be good to remember that.

Chapter 12

Devney

I had been to my fair share of weddings, but never one where I got to see the sexiest man I'd ever seen in my life standing next to the bride and groom.

Heath looked good in anything he wore, be it jeans and T-shirts, hiking gear, or nothing at all.

But a suit? A charcoal gray suit with a Tiffany blue pocket square? I nearly fell to my knees in awe of this man.

Yes, I had a problem. But wow.

As Grace and Ace said their vows, both of them with tears in their eyes, I blinked away tears of my own.

Because it was hard not to stare at Heath as they spoke. I didn't want him to think too much about my own tears. Because damn it, I had never seen something so romantic, and Heath was part of it.

By the time we hit the reception, I was giddy on my second glass of champagne.

I knew a lot of Ace's guests because I was with Heath, so it was nice to be included and not feel like I was an interloper.

I was here as Heath's date. And while some of their friends that I didn't know were giving me curious looks, they weren't rude. They just wanted to know who the girl with Heath was.

"Dustin, come over and meet Devney, my girlfriend," Heath said, and I nearly tripped.

Girlfriend.

I had called him boyfriend; it was like being in high school and wanting labels; maybe soon we would be going steady and I would have to put notes in his locker.

Not that I'd even had a locker in school because there hadn't been enough for every student at our large school. I'd just carried everything around in my backpack.

Why the heck was I thinking about that?

Maybe it was easier to think about simpler times.

This had all started as a lie. He had been a barrier so my family wouldn't worry about me.

And now, here I was, with him.

I was going to fix things with my family. I had to.

Because if I didn't, it was going to just snowball into this horrid thing.

Because if I wasn't at work, or with Addison and Paisley, I was with him.

And it was amazing.

And I needed to figure out exactly what it all meant.

"Girlfriend? I like it."

Heath squeezed my hip as Dustin beamed. "Look at you, growing up. It's wonderful to meet you, Devney. We know that you are too good for him, and we are just fine with that."

"Be nice, or I'm going to have to kick some ass," Heath grumbled.

"Seriously, when you finally figure out there are better people out there, come to me."

I just shook my head, holding back a laugh at the way Heath's eyes narrowed. "I think I am good. But thank you. Also, you have spinach in your teeth."

Dustin grinned. "The spinach puffs are amazing. Would you like me to get you some?"

Heath growled something under his breath as Luca came over and handed Dustin a toothpick.

"Clean yourself up, bro. And stop poaching on Heath's woman. She's too good for the likes of you. Hell, she's too good for all of us, but that's why we're going to keep her. Hidden and locked away."

"You're just going to lock me away?" I asked with a laugh.

"If we have to," both Heath and Luca said at the same time, before they bumped fists.

I rolled my eyes. "Well, that's a little scarier than I thought this conversation would go."

"I promise not to lock you up. I may find a way to accidentally take away your keys so you're stuck hanging out with me for a few hours, but you know, whatever."

"I wouldn't mind being stuck hanging out with you for a few hours," I said, then realized how dorky that was.

Heath pulled me to the dance floor.

"I hate dancing, so let's come out here so I can show you what moves I don't have, but at least we can get away from the guys."

He put a hand on the small of my back and gripped his other hand with mine.

"I'm not good at dancing."

"Just follow me."

"I thought you said you didn't have any moves."

His eyes went slightly smokey. "Oh, I might have lied."

We moved across the dance floor gracefully, and if I wasn't careful, I'd fall in love with him.

Other people were dancing around us, but most people had eyes for the way Heath glided across the dance floor, me in his arms.

Me. His girlfriend.

How the hell had this happened? I wasn't quite sure,

but I was really afraid if I wasn't careful, I was going to lose it all.

So, I would just cling to it. Because it wasn't a lie anymore. This wasn't fake.

This wasn't just a good time.

And that worried me more than anything.

"What is that look on your face?"

I shook my head and brought myself back to the present, grateful that he could lead so well I hadn't had to pay attention. "Where did you learn to dance like this?" I asked instead, not answering his question.

He let that slide, thankfully, and shrugged as the song changed. "One of the only good things my dad ever taught me was that to get girls, you needed to learn how to dance. So, all of us guys learned how to dance." He gestured over my shoulder, and I turned to see both Luca and August dancing with women I didn't know. They moved just like Heath, confident, with a grace that belied their size.

I looked back to Heath. "Well, I'm pretty sure you're getting the girl tonight." I winked as I said it, enjoying the way his eyes lit up.

"Damn straight." He crushed his mouth to mine. Someone cheered and Ace punched him on the shoulder.

"Hey, stop stealing the spotlight."

"Okay, I can kiss your girl too."

"I don't think so," Ace growled, even though his eyes were filled with laughter.

Carrie Ann Ryan

Heath shrugged, put both hands on Ace's cheeks, and kissed him.

I whistled and bumped Grace's shoulder as we clapped.

"Feel better?" Heath asked.

Ace fanned himself. "I feel like my heart's all atwitter. Thankfully I have my wife here to protect me." He held out his hands to Grace. "My fucking wife."

"We're going to get that tattooed on me somewhere, aren't we?" she asked with a laugh.

"Damn straight."

He pulled her into a heart-pounding kiss.

We danced more, and I was spun around the floor by Luca and August, and eventually Ace.

Everybody was having so much fun, this felt right.

By the time we got back to my place, I was exhausted but exhilarated.

Heath's mouth was on mine, and I leaned into him, wanting more.

"You're so fucking sexy," he mumbled against my lips.

"It's really hard to concentrate with your hands on my breasts." I moaned as he played with my nipples over the fabric of my dress.

"Don't worry. I'll take care of you."

"Let me take care of you this time."

Before he could disagree, I went to my knees and began undoing his belt buckle.

162

He pushed my hair back from my face, and I was glad I had taken it down from its updo.

"You don't have to do that."

"But I want to. I really, really like this."

"You like giving blowjobs?"

I blushed even as I held him in my hand, taking him out of his boxer briefs.

He groaned and shifted into my fist. I couldn't even touch my middle finger to my thumb around the base of him, but I slid my hand up and down, learning him like I did each time.

"I enjoy giving you blowjobs. I don't know if I'd enjoy it with anyone else."

"Don't talk about anyone else with my dick in your hand."

"Okay." I kissed the tip of his dick and he moaned.

"Damn. I'm going to come all over that pretty dress if we're not careful."

I let go of him and he frowned at me, until I undid the tie around my neck and stepped out of my dress.

His eyes widened.

"You weren't fucking wearing anything under that dress the whole time?"

I shrugged before I went back to my knees. I only wore my heels now, and I swallowed him whole in answer. The tip of his dick touched the back of my throat, and I breathed through my nose and swallowed just like he taught me.

He hummed, letting out curses I couldn't even understand, before he pulled at my hair and tugged me off his cock.

"Answer me, Devney. You were naked under there?"

"I couldn't wear a bra with that dress."

"And your fucking panties? Your pussy was bare the entire time?"

I shook my head and looked up at him, his cock still in my hand.

"I took them off in the car when you weren't looking. They're in my purse."

He groaned as he gently pushed my head back to his cock. I swallowed him again, playing with his balls with one hand. He shifted, bending slightly so his hands were on my breasts, plucking at my nipples. I was growing wetter and wetter with each passing moment. And when I was ready to give him more, to take all of him, he pulled away, his thighs quaking.

"Much more of that and I'm going to come down your throat."

"That's okay with me."

"Maybe. But I really want to come in that pussy of yours."

"Heath," I whispered, blushing.

"I love how you blush at me when I talk dirty, even

though you're currently naked on your knees in front of my wet dick thanks to your mouth. I'm pretty sure you can talk about sex, baby."

"Yes, but I don't know, it still makes me blush."

"Well, you're not some innocent virgin anymore. You're all mine."

I stood up and wrapped my arms around his shoulders.

He gripped my ass and lifted me up.

"Wrap your legs around me."

"I might hurt you with my heels."

"I don't fucking care."

He pressed my back against the door and slid deep inside me.

We both froze and looked down at where we connected. His cock balls-deep inside me, my pussy wet around it.

"Fuck. Condom." He began to pull out, and I tightened my inner muscles around him.

He froze, his eyes nearly crossing. "Devney."

"We were both tested. And I'm on birth control. Please. Don't leave."

"It feels so good being bare inside you. I'm not going to last long."

He ground out the words; they were barely intelligible.

"Then move. Please."

165

He slid his thumb over my clit and I came. I clenched around his cock, and then he was moving, pounding me into the wall. My breasts bounced, but he kept me from hurting my back. He was moving, kissing me and touching me. He was hard and rough and everything I craved. A craving I hadn't even known I had until I had him.

And then I was coming again, and he was filling me. He roared my name, crushed his mouth to mine, and I could barely breathe. Barely think.

I didn't want to think.

I just wanted this moment.

And everything that came with it.

Chapter 13
Devney

Today was the day.

The day I finally told the truth. A truth I should have revealed months ago. Over a *year* ago. But I'd been too wary of hurting others' feelings that I'd kept the lie up.

And now...now things felt real.

They felt too hot. Too on the edge of breaking...or *something* cataclysmic.

I hoped I wouldn't break my family's hearts.

"I can go with you."

I turned in my kitchen to see Heath sitting at the counter, coffee mug in hand.

After the incredible night after the wedding, we had slept in because we both had the day off. Heath because he and Ace had known that they would need time after the wedding, and me because Paisley had wanted me to have fun.

And while I knew both of us still had work to do, as Heath was a business owner, and my job with PR was never truly done, it was nice just to have a moment to ourselves.

He had made breakfast, which was amazing.

"Okay, now why are you smiling?" he asked, frowning at me. "Smiling thinking about me going to your family while you tell them the truth? You shouldn't have to do it alone."

I shook my head, then pulled myself out of my odd thoughts.

"I was just thinking about breakfast."

Heath leaned back in his chair, a catlike smile on his face.

"Oh, I've been thinking about my breakfast, too."

My ass on the counter, thighs spread as he knelt in front of me, and ate me out as I tried to not fall off. He made me come twice, while blueberry muffins baked in the oven. Blueberry muffins he had made from scratch.

"I was talking about the muffins," I said after a moment, finally able to get my thoughts in order. Which was sometimes very difficult when it came to Heath.

He leaned back on the bar stool, arms crossed over his chest. I wouldn't say he looked right in my kitchen. More that it felt as if he had been here for longer than he had.

What would my life have been like if my family hadn't run into the bar to confront him?

Sadder. A little more hollow.

I still didn't want to put too much into this. Because if I did, I would hurt myself in the end, and I was already going to hurt myself when I went to my family and told them the truth.

"And now you're frowning again. Let me come with you. Let me take some of the burden."

I turned on the sink to rinse my mug before I put it in the dishwasher. "No. This is my problem. It's our big family dinner, and frankly, while you are constantly invited to family dinner, I don't want to thrust you into that situation."

"You come to my family events."

"And I'm so grateful to be included." My heart did that little twist. He invited me as if I belonged there. And maybe I did. As long as I didn't think too hard about that, I was fine.

Only, it was the thinking part that always got me into trouble. Hence why I had been a virgin for so long. I was the queen of overthinking, and I got myself into situations I couldn't get out of. Hence the upcoming conversation tonight about a relationship that used to not, but now totally did exist.

"It helps that your family is somewhat contained, and I love Greer and your brothers."

I didn't say I loved him, because we weren't ready for that. I didn't know if I would ever be ready for that. That was a huge step, and it had taken me forever to get this far.

"I see, so you're ashamed of me." He gave me such a solemn look that I almost believed him, but then I saw the twinkle in his eyes.

"Heath, don't make me feel worse than I already do."

He leaned over the counter and kissed me square on the mouth. Tingles shot up my spine and I tried not to squirm. It was really hard when it came to him. Damn that man.

"Breathe. I understand that I'm invited, and it would be terrifying, but I could deal with them. At least, I hope so."

I wasn't sure, and it had nothing to do with him, but with the massive family I had.

"We would need to do flashcards and a family tree so you could get the names of everyone."

"Oh, believe me, between my sister's two men and their families? I already have a set of flashcards. I'm sure we can make one for the Johnsons."

"I think your first dinner with my family shouldn't be the dinner I explain that you lied to them the first time you met them because I lied to them for a year." I winced.

He leaned forward and gripped my hand. "Why shouldn't I be there? It's my fault too. Maybe if I let them know the truth in that moment, it wouldn't be like this."

I bit my lip as he rubbed his thumb along the fleshy part of my hand between my thumb and pointer finger.

He was always doing that, touching me without thinking. Touching to soothe.

I was getting far too used to it.

"I don't know what to do. Because if you hadn't said that, would we have still gone on a fake date?"

"There isn't anything fake about what we did last night," he teased. "Or this morning."

I blushed to the tips of my ears. "Heath."

"I'm just saying. There was nothing fake about that. Because if you were faking those orgasms, we're going to have a talk, and then I'm going to have to try harder to make you come on my face. Twice."

"Heath Cassidy, we are having a very serious conversation right now."

"Are we?" he asked, his voice going into that purr again.

Damn him.

"I need to stand up for myself. I need to just tell them. Okay?"

He moved then, coming around the counter to cup my face. His thumb brushed my cheekbone and I leaned into him. This was a problem. A major one. But one I would deal with later.

"Okay. But if they're mean to you, I'm going to kick some ass."

"They're my family. You don't get to kick their ass."

"Then you can tell them I'm very disappointed in them. How's that?" His tone was so dry that I burst out laughing.

"I still don't think you could beat the mom stare."

"I'll practice. I do have the big brother stare."

"I suppose that'll work. Now speaking of work, I know you're off, but didn't you want to go and check in to see how everyone did last night?"

He winced. "I swear I'm like a mother duck."

"I was going to say micromanager, but I kind of like the idea of you as a mother duck."

He grinned and kissed the tip of my nose. It was little things like that which were a problem.

Because I had fallen for him. I had fallen for the idea of him even when he was just a fake boyfriend. And now, with the real Heath Cassidy? Yes, I was in trouble.

We showered, thankfully quickly and not touching each other. It was hard not to touch each other when we were showering. Then he headed out. I sighed and grabbed my computer.

My text messages popped on, and I held back a laugh.

Addison: You haven't checked in after the wedding, so either you're in a ditch somewhere, or you've had some really good times with Heath. Please respond.

Paisley: Yes, please do so. And not just for work.

Though, I do like when you check in for work because I'm a micromanager.

I burst out laughing and responded.

Me: I'm alive. No ditches. Though I am exhausted.

Addison: Bragger.

Paisley: Good for you. And please don't work today. Rest up.

I snorted, shaking my head as I sat cross-legged on the couch with my laptop.

Me: I have that big family dinner tonight where I have to tell them that I'm a horrible liar.

Paisley: Keep your chin high, explain what you did, be truly sorry for it because I know you are, and make sure they understand the why of it. Even if the why may not make sense to them.

Addison: And don't let them make you feel too bad, because they need to see where they were wrong too.

I had friends here. Family. So much family that while it was overwhelming, I knew I would never be alone. I had to move past this. I had already begun to with Heath, but I needed to do this one last thing before I let myself be okay.

Me: They don't have to take my apology. I lied. I'll have to deal with the consequences.

Addison: Then they can deal with me.

Paisley: I like Addison. She's a good friend.

Addison: I love that you texted that in our group chat knowing I would see it.

Paisley: I do what I can. Now seriously, you can do this. You're strong. Stronger than you even give yourself credit for. Make sure your family remembers that.

For some reason I blinked away tears, before saying my goodbyes and checking a few emails. I needed to work on the side dish I was bringing for the night, just a quick green bean casserole with bacon. My mother loved it, and it had been my father's favorite dish on Thanksgiving. The rest of the family loved it as well, but in my head, it was part of my dad.

Maybe that was part of my problem. I was constantly trying to bring him back in my memories. To make sure I didn't forget him. To make sure he always knew I would never forget him. Maybe putting up that wall made everyone so eager to tear it down to be with me.

I needed to be better. I needed to stop being so selfish. And I needed to stand up for myself.

So I would.

And I had to hope I didn't screw up.

Dinner at my family's house was always an event. We didn't always have all of us there, since finding a day of the month when every single person was off work, in town, and not doing any of the thousands of things that we do as humans was almost impossible. However, tonight, all of my siblings, their spouses, and kids would be there.

So of course, tonight would be the best and only time to deal.

I would not freak out.

I hoped.

"What's wrong?" Maureen asked as soon as she looked at me.

My eldest stepsister, and one of my greatest friends in the world, hugged me. "You seem stressed. Is it work? Heath? The weather?"

"Maureen, darling, please give your sister a moment to breathe. You're overwhelming her."

My mom nudged Maureen away before bringing me in for a hug. "And I see you brought the casserole! Thank you so much."

Elizabeth took it from my hands as Andy took his turn to hug me and kissed me on the forehead. Paige slid through and kissed me on my cheek while Lee took my other cheek.

When the stepsibs were done, their spouses came in, each hugging me in turn, the kids swarming me when it was their turn. At one point I held an infant that I was pretty sure was Lee's, but then I realized it might have been Andy's.

I swear we all needed name tags, and I was part of the family.

And then my half-siblings, Russ, Kennedy, Virginia, Heather, and Justice, each hugged me in turn, before updating me all at once about their latest issues in school, sports, and something about a video game that had just released.

And, thankfully, I knew what they were talking about, because I tried to keep up to date with everybody's lives, so I sat down with them and listened as they explained the new tokens that were going to ruin the update of the game.

"You don't understand. They went through all of this with the $29.99 price of a game, where each of us has to buy our own versions instead of just playing as a different character."

I nodded as Russ explained the game to me.

"So, each of us paid for our own versions of the game, and we have to play on different consoles, or we overwrite each other."

"Well, that sounds a little greedy," I grumbled, thinking about the sheer cost of it.

"Thankfully, we found a way around that by playing on the cloud on different games. But still, it's a little confusing, and I'm always afraid I'm going to overwrite something," Virginia said.

"But that's not even the worst part. Now they're going

to charge you for tokens to get things that you want even after the game. It's all just a money grab, and I hate it."

"Me too." Justice agreed with Heather, as they both folded their arms over their chest exactly like I did.

I frowned, trying to figure out how to fix it, and then realized I had no idea how to fix it. Literally, there was nothing I could do, other than listen to them and try to be the best big sister I could.

"Are you having fun with the game at least?"

Russ shook his head. "I was, but now it's getting boring because they just want you to pay for everything."

"I don't know. We did spend the initial money up front. Now it's lost."

I squeezed Kennedy's hand. "Okay. So you spent the money up front using your allowance." Each of them nodded. "And you had a lot of fun for what, a few weeks?"

"Almost three whole months," Heather clarified.

"Okay, well I think that's good. I wish it was longer, but maybe you can come back to it after they work the kinks out, and maybe they'll realize they can't charge you for every single little thing."

"And what if they realize they can always charge you?" Justice, my youngest sibling asked.

"Then you find a game that you can play together that doesn't charge you individually."

"Good luck with that in this day and age," my stepdad said as he came in and kissed the top of my head. "What happened to the days where we just played a board game?"

"We still play those," my mom said as she squeezed her husband's hand. "The problem is that there's not a board game big enough for all of us.

"And we're not allowed to play Monopoly anymore," Maureen said dryly.

I rolled my eyes. "Not after 'the incident.'"

Maureen narrowed her gaze at me. "I thought we were never going to bring up 'the incident.'"

"We only ended up in the emergency room once while playing Monopoly. And I don't know why that's 'the incident,' and Candy Land isn't," Lee said.

"What's 'the incident?'" Lee's wife asked, and he shook his head. "We must not speak of it."

"Maureen didn't mean to stab her sister."

Elizabeth rubbed her arm where she still had a small scar. "I didn't even know you could be stabbed by a thimble until that day."

"My poor baby," Elizabeth's wife said as she kissed her cheek.

I held back a laugh and tried not to look at my mother, until we all burst out laughing.

"We need to stop thinking of 'the incident.'"

"Wait, does that mean more people were stabbed in Candy Land than in Monopoly?" one of the spouses asked, and my stepfather held out his hands.

"We will not speak of it again. Not if we want peace in our time."

"This is why we have different board games in each part of the room during game days. Or we have a game that we make up that can handle fifty of us."

"I don't think anything could handle us," Mom said as she snuggled into William.

I smiled at the two of them. I was so happy she had William. He loved my mom with everything he had.

And my mom loved him just as much. I knew she would always love my father. But she had the capacity to love so many people, to bring them into her heart, that it put mine to shame.

She opened her heart for the children of William's first marriage, and I tried to do the same. I thought it worked. They were my siblings and I loved them. The only reason that I even called them the steps was so I could group those five versus the other five. There were just so many that they needed nicknames.

But they were my family. My siblings. My brothers and sisters that I loved with all my heart.

I needed to just get this out there.

My mom frowned at me, pulling me out of my thoughts.

"Baby? What's wrong?"

At that, everyone went quiet and looked at me, worry etched on their faces. Sadly, it was the same worry that had been on their faces when they were trying to set me up on countless dates, afraid that I would be all alone and never start the next phase of my life.

It was this space that caused me to blurt out the lie in the first place.

Now I needed to make up for it, and I tried to find some backbone.

"I have something to tell you, and it sucks, and I don't want you to hate me, okay?"

I said that so quickly that everybody immediately tried to reassure me.

"We love you, just talk to us," Elizabeth said softly.

She held her wife's hand, while their free hands each held one of their children.

Everybody was so wonderful, I needed to get this over with.

"It's about Heath."

"Did he hurt you?" my brother asked, and I shook my head.

"No. Stop. Just let me get through this, and you'll understand why. At least I hope you will. Heath and I just started dating."

"Well, I guess it could feel new. And like forever all at the same time, right?" one of my sisters asked.

I shook my head, and realized I needed to be more clear. "No, over a year ago when you kept pestering me about dating." Maureen opened her mouth to say something, and I realized that using the word "pestering" probably wasn't going to help.

"I mean, when everybody was worried about me finding a match and wanted to set me up, and afraid that I was never going to find my happy ever after, and you guys were really worried about me, and I was fine. I really was. But I didn't know how to make you stop."

My mother frowned at me. "Did we make you feel like you had no other choice?"

And my mother knew, just like that. She knew, because she knew everything about me. But I needed to make it clear for everyone else.

"I lied. When everybody kept asking me over and over again when I was going to start dating and kept trying to set me up with friends and trying to get me on apps because you were so afraid I was going to die a virgin." I winced. "Sorry," I said, and my mom shook her head.

"No, keep going.

"I lied. I made up a boyfriend. Only, I couldn't think of a fake one, so I made up a guy who smiled at me at a bar. I hadn't even stepped foot in that bar again until the day you guys went to him, because I was so embarrassed about lying that he was mine."

Everybody was silent for a moment, then Maureen frowned, an odd expression on her face. "And when we went to confront him, did he know ahead of time?"

I shook my head. "No. He didn't. I have no idea why

he went along with it, but he said he wanted to protect me."

"From us," my sister said softly.

I nodded, feeling horrible.

"And then it turned into something real. And I think I'm falling in love with him." I hadn't meant to say that part. That was just for me, but maybe I should tell them more. Because I was hurting them.

And I needed to make up for it. Perhaps baring my soul would help.

"I'm so sorry. I didn't know how to tell you. That I was fine with the way that I was. That I liked working as hard as I was. That I wasn't really good at talking to guys. I know it makes me sound like a coward. And I feel like one sometimes. But I didn't want to continue to lie. I love all of you. I love how we are big and messy and loud. I just didn't know how to fix it."

"Because we were so pushy."

This again was Maureen, as if she was the spokesperson for them all.

I wiped away tears, unaware until then I was even crying.

"You are. But we all are."

"But we didn't make up boyfriends to keep you off our backs." She let out a hollow laugh. "And I suppose us showing up en masse to go confront that boyfriend just reinforced who we were. The bullies who want what they think is best for their little sister. And couldn't even see that she was happy enough before we forced her to lie." Maureen walked out at that, but not before I'd seen the tears. Her husband followed, as did Elizabeth.

I pressed my lips together, waiting for someone to say anything. My stepfather raised his hand.

"Thank you for telling us. So, you're falling for Heath?" he asked, and I smiled, before bursting into tears and running from the room. I needed a moment. I had hurt my sister. I had hurt a lot of them. And I didn't know what I was supposed to do.

A hand touched my shoulder and I turned to see my mother there, a sad expression on her face. "Devney?"

"I am such an idiot. I made up a boyfriend for a year, and then it turns out I'm falling in love with the real version of him. I don't know what rom-com tropes I've hit, but it's a little on point."

My mom laughed. "It's okay, you know. We are pushy. Heck, I think we've interrogated all of the spouses, and then of course we had to interrogate you until you had to make up a partner. We love you so much."

"I know you do."

"Good. I've always done my best to make sure you knew that you are part of this family. I fell in love with those kids as soon as I became their stepmother. Before, even. I always wanted a big family, and I wasn't lucky enough to have one with your father before fate took him from us. But then fate gave me another family, and even more after that. Between marrying into the family with William's children, you, and then having your younger siblings, I have eleven. And I always wanted to make sure that you never felt that you were stuck in the middle."

"I promise I know you all love me. And I love the loudness and being part of everything. I love the text chains and knowing that I'm never alone. I just sometimes don't know how to speak up over the noise. I'm doing better. I'm trying. I do it for work, I don't know why I can't do it with family."

My mom pushed my hair back from my face and smiled at me. "I love you. And I get it. And honestly, I kind of knew."

I blinked. "Excuse me?"

"You were so good about keeping Heath out of the conversation, always deflecting. We just wanted what was best for you, but we didn't listen. So I let you have your imaginary boyfriend. I know you think you lied, and maybe you did, but you were protecting yourself. Maureen will get over it. Because she's not mad at you. She's upset with herself for not seeing it."

"I know. Maureen is amazing. I never have to fight the world because I'll know she'll be right beside me."

"And sometimes she'll stand right in front of you and try to fight your battles, even when you don't want her to."

"I'll apologize again."

"Maybe, if you need to. The rest of us are just happy that you're happy now. And you are happy with Heath, right?"

I pressed my lips together, playing with my fingers. "I think so? I don't know. How do you know if you're in love?"

My mom smiled then, her eyes going dreamy. "I have been blessed to be in love twice in my life. Twice I have found men who are worthy of who I am and who my family is. Twice I have tried to come up with words for what that feeling is, and I can't. I hate just saying that you just know. There's a spark inside you that you're scared of. There's this part where you want to be with them every moment, but also know that you need some time apart. There's a part of you that knows that your life is forever altered, and you can see a future—even if it scares the hell out of you. That's what love is, it's the fear and the anxiety and the hope and the angst and the passion and the dreams that come with that person. I've been lucky twice. And I really hope you're lucky with Heath."

I wiped away tears, once again unaware when I started crying. "That's so beautiful, Mom."

"I see it in you. That fear and that hope. Bring him by next time. The family will get over it, even if I don't think there's anything for them to get over."

"I should still apologize."

"And we should apologize to you for sometimes

forgetting that we're allowed a moment of pause. Of quietness. We're not quite good at that."

"No. But I don't mind it. I like the noise."

As if on cue, somebody in the house screamed, laughing over a game upturned.

My mom just rolled her eyes and held me close.

"So, tell me everything about Heath again. I want to know exactly what it is about this boy."

My heart did that aching thing again, and I wondered if that was love, or maybe just the fear part. "I don't know, Mom. I don't quite know how he feels about me."

"Well, he's an idiot if he doesn't love you."

"Mom."

"I'm just telling you the truth. As a mom and woman, I know."

"Can we talk about anything else?"

"Maybe. But come on, it's family dinner. And you're family, Devney. Wrapped up in the middle."

She kissed my forehead and I followed her in, leaning into Maureen as she hugged me without another word.

I had messed up, and maybe so had they. But we would be okay. Because we were family.

Of course, though, that only left the worry about what exactly I felt for Heath.

And how on earth I could figure out what he felt for me.

Chapter 14
Devney

"So as you slide your hands up and down the shaft, you're going to want to make sure you have control."

I pressed my lips together and did my best not to laugh. I could feel Heath's knee shaking next to me, and I knew he was holding back a laugh too, and we were about to fail. However, it was the guy on the other side of us who burst out laughing and held up his hand as the instructor scowled at him.

"Sorry. Sometimes I am a twelve-year-old boy. I promise I'm going to do my best and not break this vase."

"You've got strong hands, I'm sure you can figure it out." The instructor said it in such a no-nonsense tone that I was pretty sure she didn't even realize the double entendre.

In fact, everything we were doing in this class tonight seemed to be a double entendre.

"Am I making a bowl or a vase?" Heath asked from beside me, and I looked at the lump of clay between his very strong hands and forgot the question for a moment.

"I think we were going for vase, but I might end up with a bowl. Or a lopsided thingamabob."

"Well, at least we're trying. Maybe. Though if I burst out laughing, will she murder us?"

I winced. "Maybe."

The instructor let us talk amongst ourselves as we worked, and I threw another pot.

"I really have no idea what I'm doing."

"Same. And I didn't realize it was so messy."

I looked over at him, at the speck of mud on his cheek, and grinned. "But you look cute."

"Thanks. That's what I was going for."

"Are you having fun at least?"

Heath grinned at me and winked. "Yeah, I am. How did you think of this place?"

I shrugged, screwed up the pot, and started over. "It was on a quiz thing."

Heath laughed.

"Let me guess, what to do on your fourth date?"

"I think it's like our eighth or something."

"Or more. I like that we don't keep count anymore."

"Thank God, because I have enough in my head right

now with work and family that I don't really want to remember an exact number."

But we were on date fourteen. Not that I was going to say that out loud.

"Plus, we wanted a place that was not based around alcohol, since you own a bar, and not a place that Paisley owned part of because she seems to be taking over the world. It sort of narrowed it down."

"The whole city of Denver, and here we are."

He winked as he said it.

We had been busy lately, me with three different PR nightmares, and him with an inspection and inventory. He had also had three different events at his bar, so we barely had time to see each other.

I had spoken to my family every day since our dinner, but things still felt awkward. I had hurt them. I knew I had, and while they had also hurt me, I was the one who'd lied. They just pushed. And I hoped we had found a way to get through it.

We finished our bowls-turned-pots-turned-vases and set them off to the side so they could go into the kiln. We were allowed to come back to another class to glaze them, or just pick them up as is. I wasn't sure I wanted to see my creation again. It had been a fun date, but it wasn't great.

Heath just kept laughing and I pushed at his shoulder. "Yours looks like a beautiful even bowl. Mine has a hole in it."

"It was a handle."

"At the bottom?" I asked, and he just kept laughing. "You're mean."

"I can't help it. This was your idea."

"So, I guess we'll never be one of those couples that gets a pottery wheel in the garage?"

"We can always reenact that scene from that old movie, *Ghost*."

"I've never seen that movie, but I have seen that scene."

"Yeah, we could try that. Though maybe it might be a little too obscene for us."

He took my hand as we walked through the park towards his truck. It was a lovely night, people out enjoying dinner, children playing in the fields and at the park. And there were a bunch of college guys playing soccer in one of the far-off fields. Most weren't even wearing shoes, they were just laughing and enjoying themselves. When the ball suddenly flew at my face, Heath moved quickly. I didn't even have time to panic before he jumped in front of it and used his shoulder to knock it down.

"Sorry about that. Got away from me. Are you okay?" one of the guys asked as he pushed his beachy waves back from his face.

"I'm good. You?" Heath asked, and I nodded, touching my sandal to the ball.

"I'm really okay. I'm glad that Heath was so quick."

"Me too. And glad that it didn't go towards those kids. Sorry, again." The guy blushed, and Heath cleared his throat.

"No problem."

"You want to join us?" another guy asked, but he wasn't looking at Heath. No, he was looking at me. I frowned as Heath narrowed his gaze, but then I kicked the ball.

"It's been a while since I played soccer. But I can try."

"Okay, now I want to see what those legs can do," Heath said. I took off my sandals and, even though I was wearing a sundress, I figured I could play for a few minutes. Heath was wearing nicer black shoes so he kicked them off as well, and we were off.

We ended up on different teams, with Heath as the midfielder, me as a forward. Soon I was running across the field, kicking the ball towards the net. I missed the first time, but then we were laughing and I was jumping over a fallen teammate to try for another goal. It slid between the posts and everybody cheered. Heath picked me up and twirled me around.

"That was beautiful."

"Wow, that's some skill," one of the women on my team said.

She held out her hand and we high-fived before she pulled me in for a quick hug, then went off to go kiss her boyfriend—who happened to be the goalie I just scored on.

"Okay, that was the hottest thing I've ever seen," Heath said as he took my hand, and we waved our good-byes to everyone.

"I played in middle school and high school, but not college. I wasn't good enough."

"You were good enough against those college guys."

I rolled my eyes. "I never played with college dudes when I was in college."

We let the double meaning slide.

"Well, you're mine now."

The way he said it made me let out a shuddering breath and take his hand, letting the sunset dance over us.

"Tonight was nice."

"Yeah. Good to take a moment."

"My mom invited you to family dinner. When you're ready."

"We can make that happen. Speaking of, our family dinner's on Thursday if you want to join us."

I squeezed his hand, trying my best to keep my heart in line.

It wouldn't be good to blurt out my feelings, not when everything felt so smooth, so nice. I didn't know what Heath wanted and, frankly, I didn't know what I wanted. So it would be good to keep my feelings inside for now.

"Just let me know what I need to bring."

"I know you work long hours," he began, but I cut him off.

"So do you. I don't know if I could run a bar."

"I don't know if I could run an entire PR arm of a company."

"Well, good thing we are situated how we are. We're good at what we do individually."

"And I guess we're pretty good when we come together," Heath said with a wink.

"Nice line."

"I've been practicing them."

"They better be just for me."

"You know it."

We made our way back to his house, and before I knew it, his mouth was on mine.

He was just so potent, so everything.

"Would you like something to drink?" he asked as he pulled away and I tried to catch my breath.

"No, I really just need you."

I didn't tell him the depth of that statement, but I had a feeling he could sense it.

We were on the precipice of something, but I didn't want to go too far. For him to see too much. So I went to my tiptoes and kissed him again.

He picked me up in one quick motion. So damn strong. It made me feel small and taken care of.

He walked me back to the bedroom and gently set me

down.

"I want you."

I swallowed hard and trailed my fingers up his chest.

"I want you, too."

"Do you want to try something new tonight?" he asked, his voice low and full of promise.

I swallowed hard, pressing my thighs together. "How new?"

"I promise I'll be gentle."

He slid his hands over my ass, and then pulled my dress up. I was wearing a thong, so his hand brushed against my skin, cupping my cheek. And then he slid between my cheeks, over me.

I swallowed hard. "Oh."

He grinned and kissed me harder.

"I've used my fingers, but what about something else?"

"Are you sure I'm ready for that?"

He chuckled low.

"Maybe a toy? To see if you like it?"

I had surely liked it when it was just his fingers, so I nodded.

"Yes, please."

His mouth was on me again and I groaned. Somehow my dress was on the floor, my panties quickly following. I hadn't worn a bra, so I kicked off my sandals. He had me on my back on the bed and was hovering over me. I pulled off his shirt, drooling at the sight of him, sliding my fingers over the thin layer of chest hair, and then down over the hard ridges of his abdomen. He was so beautiful, so damn sexy. It was all I could do not to come at just the look of him. And the feel of his jeans against my naked body was a contrast of desire that I hadn't known I ever wanted. I wanted him. I needed him. And it was going to take every ounce of control not to tell him how much I loved him. I wasn't ready for that. Not when we were just figuring things out.

He slid his hands between my thighs, parting my folds as his middle finger slid over my clit, sending a shock through me. He kept kissing me, and then slid down a bit more, his mouth on my nipples. He sucked on them, one at a time, biting gently down on the tightened buds. When he slid his finger deep inside me, I arched into him. One hand in his hair, the other digging into the muscles of his shoulder as he continued to finger fuck me. One finger, then another. And then he slowly slid his finger out of me and used my juices to slide between my cheeks. When he probed my back entrance, I tensed.

"I can stop."

"No, I'm ready. I really like when you do that," I said, my voice barely above a whisper as I could feel the heat of my blush across my skin.

He looked so damn proud of himself, as he continued to work on me, gently pressing against my entrance. He

Carrie Ann Ryan

moved then, leaving me bereft when he went to the night-stand to pull out a few things. There was a quick snap of a bottle as he opened the lube and spread it between my legs. I shivered at the touch. And then he knelt between my legs and looked down at me.

"You're like a fucking goddess. So beautiful."

"Heath. I need you."

"You've got me."

I wanted to see more into that, but I couldn't, not then. Not when he had a plug in his hand.

"This has a flared base. I'm going to gently guide it inside you, but what you need to do is push back. Relax and then push out and it'll slide right in. The flared base will keep you safe."

"Is that a bright pink jewel at the end?" I asked, nervous.

"I've never used this before. It's small and just for you. Everything is just for you, Devney."

Then he was kissing me again, bringing me to the edge of bliss one more time. When I felt the cool pressure against my back entrance, I tensed for a moment, until his hand was on my clit, bringing me back to the sensation of warmth and need. Then there was a slight burn as he began to press it inside, and I did as he instructed. It was so much, so full, and I could barely hold back, and then it was inside of me and I was shaking, needing more, not knowing what I needed at all.

196

"It's so beautiful. You're so beautiful."

And then he was over me, touching me again. Just one swipe of his fingers along my clit and I came, the sensation different than anything before. My pussy clenched around his fingers, and my ass clenched around the plug. It didn't make any sense, it was too much, it was not enough, I just needed him. I scratched at his arms, needing more. I didn't have any words. But then he was there, and he was sliding deep inside of me. I was even fuller than before. His cock was so big, stretching me, but then the plug was also pressing deep inside me.

He was moving slow, easy, and then harder and faster. I met him thrust for thrust. When he pulled out of me again and set me on all fours, I knew it was so he could see the jewel.

I wiggled my ass for him, loving the way that he chuckled roughly, before he spread my cheeks and slammed into my pussy. He kept thrusting, slapping my ass once, twice. The burn was so much, so desirable, that I came again, and this time he groaned, holding onto my hips with a bruising force as he pummeled into me and followed me into his own orgasm.

He draped himself over me, holding me tight, as we both came back down to earth.

That had been the singular most erotic experience of my life, and it was only just beginning, because he was still touching me.

Carrie Ann Ryan

I had fallen in love with Heath Cassidy long before this moment.

But now I craved him. He was my sensation, my drug.

And I knew the withdrawal would break me.

So maybe, just maybe, I would never let go.

198

Chapter 15

Heath

"Seriously, there was an actual octopus tattoo."

I set my beer down, grateful I hadn't taken a drink while Luca was telling this story.

"And she just took off her pants in the middle of your office to show you?" August asked.

"Should I leave the room for this?" Greer asked, from where she sat pressed against Devney's side.

"Maybe we both should leave the room."

"No, it wasn't like that. She just unzipped her pants."

"Seriously, don't tell me," Greer said, holding up both hands.

"It was just right over her underwear, I swear, I sort of made this high-pitched scream noise and ran out of the room carrying two puppies."

I burst out laughing, imagining Luca looking scared to

death of a woman undressing in the middle of his office. I didn't blame him though, that wasn't a situation I wanted to get in the middle of, unless it was Devney, of course.

"Oh my gosh. I would've paid to see that."

"It was embarrassing as hell. I still can't believe she did that."

"So she just took off her pants for you, without you asking her to?" Devney asked.

"I asked her what she meant by Release the Kraken, since she named her puppies after other pieces of lore. Then she needed to show me. And now my life is turning a new direction."

"And I bet your office partner was laughing his head off," August put in.

Luca shook his head. "Pretty much. He'll be taking care of her from now on. Mostly because I ran and screamed in such an embarrassing fashion."

"At least you weren't taking advantage of her," Greer said.

"I would never."

She shook her head. "I meant, at least other people won't think you were taking advantage of her. I know you wouldn't. My brothers are pretty good guys."

I looked over at Greer and smiled. I didn't know when it happened, but we all just sort of clicked. Maybe it was time, maybe it was including Greer's men and Devney in dinners like this so it wasn't just the four of us. We were still getting to know one another. I wasn't the best at the whole family thing, but I was learning. It was hard not to want more with Devney though, even if things with her family were a little awkward right now in her eyes.

But hell, all of our families were a little unusual, but it finally seemed as if we were learning how to become a huge family.

I was forever grateful that we were making it work.

"Anyway, after I screamed, the rest of the staff took care of her, I finished the examination of the puppies, and then I helped a sick turtle."

"Do you ever help with large animals or just household ones?"

"When I was in school, we went out to a few of the ranches in eastern Oregon. But I'm not a large animal vet. I could be in a pinch, but that's a whole other specialty. My lab partner in school actually is a large animal veterinarian. They help with breach cows, horses that work the ranch, the rodeo, and even Thoroughbred racehorses."

"And you get the puppies and kittens," August put in.

"I am fine with the puppies and kittens. If you guys are looking for some though, I can always find you a good match."

"If they wouldn't make me break out into hives, you know I would," I commented.

"I know, still though, maybe we could try a parakeet?"

"You have a parakeet?" Devney asked.

"His name is Bob. He doesn't like other birds."

I shook my head and leaned back into the couch as Devney sank against me, and we listened to Luca and August tell stories about their jobs. I guess a vet and a high school science teacher sometimes had similar stories.

Everything just felt nice. Like we had been doing this forever. Like we hadn't lost so much time together.

I was so damn happy.

The way Greer was with her men, how caring they were for her, and how easily she got along with them, I felt like maybe we could make this work. She was the example all of us needed.

Maybe Devney and I could do something like that. And wasn't that a scary thought.

"Anyway, we made dessert, if you're interested," Greer put in.

"You made dessert? Or you brought it over from your bakery?" Luca asked, and then he ducked her fist.

"Greer, you're getting better about not breaking your thumb as you hit," August said.

"Like we'd let our girl punch awkwardly like that," Ford said, shaking his head.

I set my beer down and whispered to my girl, "Having fun?"

"Yes. You guys are hilarious."

"We try. You just let me know when you want to head out. I know you have an early morning tomorrow."

"I'm fine. I'm just sad I couldn't force Addison to come. She could have used the laughter."

"Everything going okay over there?" I asked.

I was worried about Addison, too, though I wasn't sure of the details.

"I don't know. She's not talking to me about it. She's just so busy. I know she gets along with all of you, so it helps her relax."

"Only she's not relaxing."

"Nope. And then of course there's the other part of our trio, one I don't want to name in this room."

I nodded, grateful that August wasn't paying attention to us. The growing friendship between Paisley and Devney might become an issue one day. Everybody seemed to be okay with it now, to either ignore the situation or just to move past it. But I had a feeling that things would come to a head at some point. I didn't want Devney to get caught in the middle.

The doorbell rang at that moment and I frowned, looking over at August. "Were you expecting someone?"

August stood up, as it was his night to host, but I still got up with him. We took turns between the four of us.

My brother frowned. "I got it. I don't know who it could be, though. Maybe it's my neighbor, annoyed that I left the trash cans out yesterday."

"HOAs, man, they kill you," Luca said.

But for some reason, an uneasy feeling settled over me and I followed my twin toward the door.

"Let's just see who it is," August said in a low tone, then he looked through the peephole and cursed under his breath. "Well hell. I didn't realize the lawyer gave them our address." I knew exactly who it was. "Too late to shut off the lights and pretend we're not here." When August opened the door, I wasn't surprised to see who it was.

Our parents stood there, all tanned from their cruise, looking in love, sappy and happy. Our parents. Two people we didn't really know. Who had broken our family more than once but hadn't even had the decency to realize it.

"My boys. My sweet boys." My mother reached out to us, the same mother who hadn't raised us, who hadn't wanted us at all. I took a step back. "My twins. I'm so happy you're alive, Heath. We could have lost you, you know. We're so lucky that August was just fine. At least we had one healthy twin during that terrible time."

"What are you guys doing here?" I asked because I knew August wouldn't. He would just close the door in their face and walk away. Which was what I should have done. Her random statement was par for the course. They never cared that they hurt us. Or that August hurt too while I was sick. I might be healthy now, but I'd almost died. And my parents used that time to fight with each other.

And while that could make sense, and was something I wanted to do now, we weren't alone.

My mom didn't even have the decency to look ashamed. Ashamed for what she had done to us or that she hadn't even been in my life. She'd walked away without a second thought.

She and our father had ripped apart our family and didn't seem to fucking care.

"Son, it's good to see you," Dad said as he moved forward.

I took another step back, shaking my head. "Again, what are you guys doing here?"

Mom beamed, ignoring my words. Ignoring *me* like usual "We wanted to see our children. And with all the cars out front, I assume you're all here? It's so nice that you are getting together. The whole family. Is Greer here?"

"Mom?" Greer asked.

I turned to see my baby sister standing there, eyes wide, surprise on her face.

"My baby. I'm so sorry that I haven't been able to see you or meet your men. Are they here? Look at you, getting it all with two men. I knew it would take two to handle you. You were always so fierce when you were a kid." Then Julia Cassidy was clutching Greer, while Greer just stood there, hands still at her sides. Noah and Ford came out, scowls on their faces.

I met their gazes, and didn't know what to say. There was no getting out of this, no fixing it.

We were screwed.

Luca came over then too, feet dragging, and he wasn't alone. Devney was at his side. Devney, my girlfriend, was about to see exactly where we had come from. And why I wanted nothing to do with this.

"Oh, you're all here, that's so wonderful." My mother stepped forward, but Luca took a step back.

"I didn't know you were in town," I said, bringing the attention back to me. I wasn't about to let Luca get hurt by my mother again. She and my father had done enough to him.

"Well, we just got back. Before we go out again, and well, since we had August's address, we thought we'd stop by."

"With no warning," August added.

"We don't need warning for family, do we?" Dad asked, and Gerald Cassidy did what he did best. He put on a bright smile and turned towards Devney.

"And who does this beautiful woman belong to? Is she with you, Greer? Are you making a full poly knot with your two men?"

How my parents even knew what those words meant, I didn't care. They were trying to be open, caring for their daughter, as they never once had before this.

I took a step forward and put myself between Greer, Devney, and my parents.

"What do you guys want?" I asked.

"Why are you being so rude?" My mom shook her head and moved around me.

"Hello, I'm Julia Cassidy, and this is my husband, Gerald Cassidy."

Devney looked around, and then at my mother's outstretched hand. Devney was sweet, polite, so she shook my mother's hand, and then my father's. "Hi, I'm Devney."

"Devney, that is a wonderful name. And who are you here with?"

"Oh. Um." Devney cleared her throat. "I'm here with Heath."

My mother looked at me and grinned. "Oh. Our Heath. Our eldest boy. He's so strong, isn't he? Well, if he's anything like his dad, you're going to want to keep an eye on him." She winked as she said it, and it took me a few moments to catch on to what she was saying.

My dad rolled his eyes. "It was only one time."

"Last month. But it's okay. You're going to love him no matter what. They have addictions, you know. They stray, but then you bring them back."

"Straying is the fun part. Because then you get to make up." My dad tugged at my mom's hair and kissed her, far too hard and intimately for where they were.

I pinched the bridge of my nose as we all stood there in silence.

What was there to say when it came to our parents?

There was nothing funny about the parent trap situation they had put us in and there was nothing funny about what they were doing now.

"Anyway, we came to see your restaurant."

"I own a bar."

"Oh. Well, I thought maybe it was like a café or diner or something."

"I own the café and coffee shop, Mom," Greer said.

"All entrepreneurs." Then she turned to August. "And Aggie, how is elementary school treating you?"

"It's August. I don't go by that name." And my twin taught high school, not that our parents knew that.

Mom didn't seem to care. "Oh shush. I'm your mother."

August growled. "Are you?"

"Oh stop. I've always been your mother."

I stepped forward, done with this. "You know, I'm not in the mood for this family drama. His name is August, and he teaches high school. You would know that if you cared about your kids. But you don't."

"I have always been your mother."

"To *me*. When you felt like it," Greer added.

"Why are you guys so mean to us? Don't you care that your father and I love each other and we're finally back together? We're a family again. And look at all of you. You have grown so close. Just like I always knew you would."

My parents were fucking delusional. Nothing about what they had done when we were children made sense, and it was even worse now.

I just wanted this to end.

"You guys should go," I said, because even though it wasn't my house, August looked like he wanted to hit someone. He was just so fucking angry all the time, and I was supposed to be the cool one. The calm one. But it wasn't going to work.

Luca looked at them, and I knew the pain in his gaze, and I knew why. I knew what they had done, and what he had lost. What my sister had lost.

I was done.

"Well, I just wanted to let you know that we're in town for a bit."

I ignored my mother and glared at my father. "Is there anything else you wanted?"

"You were always so ungrateful. I took care of you, you know. When you were sick, and we spent all that money to make you better. And when August was so clingy because you were sick and he wasn't. We spent money on him, too. And Luca...well, we always did so much for him and *her*. Then Greer? She had everything she wanted. I made sure you were good men. Strong. Not sissies."

"That's enough," I said as I gestured towards the door. "If you're going to be fucking bigots, you can leave."

My father looked wide-eyed over at Noah and Ford. "That's not what I meant."

Noah smirked and Ford didn't say a word. He didn't have to, with the look of death and anger on his face.

"It's fine. We know what you meant."

We all did.

"Thanks for showing us that you guys are together again; let us know when the next divorce hits you on your asses," August growled, and my parents shook their heads.

"So ungrateful. Don't you know that we showed you what love was? That it was hard. But you could always find a way."

They kept talking, but I ignored them as August pushed them out. I stood silent next to Devney.

Because there was nothing else to say.

My parents were fucking ridiculous. They were the example of what we shouldn't do in relationships.

I only had fling after fling, one-night stand after one-night stand. I was barely holding this family together as it was. And from the way it looked as if we were all ready to bolt, I wasn't doing a good job.

Luca said something, and Greer let out a hollow laugh before Noah and Ford mentioned that they needed to get home.

I just stood there next to Devney, and I knew what I needed to do.

Devney needed someone that knew what he was doing. That actually had a future. That didn't have the craziness of his parents in his past. I really wished I knew how to fix that. How to be good enough for her.

Because I wasn't.

"Heath?" she finally spoke into the darkness, her voice soft.

I couldn't look at her, not with the taint of what just happened still on me. "Meet the Cassidys. Well, you always knew we were fun. Now you see where we get it from."

Luca was gone already, and I didn't even see him go. I nodded at August and we left before dessert was even served.

Devney didn't have anything to say. She just held my hand, trying to comfort me.

There was nothing to comfort. That was just where I came from. There was no fixing it. But I could at least fix something.

Before I broke it in the first place.

Chapter 16
Devney

I added garlic to the already hot pan with my onions wilting, and hoped I wasn't going to burn them today. I burned garlic fifty percent of the time, even though it was my favorite thing in the world. Tonight was just my version of a quick dinner, some onions and garlic, add some champagne baby tomatoes, and then put it over pasta. Maybe I'd add another vegetable if I was in the mood, but tomatoes counted. Okay, they were a fruit, but they counted.

I hummed along to the music, shaking my ass in my short shorts and tank top. I was hot, exhausted, and had had a full workday that lasted until 7:00 p.m. and I *still* had things to do. I knew Paisley was running around doing a hundred things as well. I loved my job. I loved dealing with clients and trying to find the best ways to get the word out there. What I hated was when one client decided to go off script and then we had to fire them. Sometimes there was no saving the situation, there was only trying to ease some of the hurt caused. But I wasn't going to focus on that, I was going to eat real food, not just a granola bar, and use up some of the produce in my refrigerator before it went bad. Because I had been spending so much time with Heath, I hadn't spent enough time at home to have groceries.

I quickly stirred the pasta to make sure it didn't stick to the bottom of the pot, and then went back to sautéing the garlic and onions.

Dinner a couple of nights ago had been awkward. At first, it was wonderful. As if I had fit in, and this was my future. My everything.

It almost didn't seem real.

But then his parents had shown up and everything changed.

I hadn't known what to say. I didn't think anyone had. Ford and Noah tried to protect Greer, but she had stood in front of them, wanting to stand up for herself. I wasn't sure how they had been able to hold back from doing something to her parents. But they had bundled her up and escaped with her as soon as possible.

I knew what their parents had done, splitting up the family constantly. But I didn't know the details. I didn't know why Luca looked like he was going to throw up, why August was so angry.

But I did know Heath thought the responsibility was on his shoulders. Even if that wasn't the truth. He felt that way. I hadn't been able to help. He kissed me on the cheek and said he needed to go back and check on August, and that he would call me.

Instead of sleeping together, talking through it, and letting me try to help, he walked away.

And he hadn't called.

I swallowed hard but continued to stir, adding the tomatoes. They would wilt, and then I'd be able to pop them to make my own version of sauce. I added some fresh parsley, because I had a plant that I hadn't killed yet, and bit my lip, wondering if I should have done something different. I hadn't called him, but I had texted, and he'd replied with a short message that he was okay. But it didn't seem like enough. I knew how families could be. I knew things were complicated and sometimes you couldn't fix everything. But it still felt like I was making a mistake. That I wasn't doing enough.

Because he was hurt, and I wanted to help. And even though I knew I couldn't do much, I wanted to help him.

Because I loved him. And I wanted to keep loving him.

Once everything was ready, I drained the pasta, added a little pasta water to my sauce, and then topped the pasta with the tomato medley. It wasn't perfect, and I was pretty sure I hadn't added enough oregano, but it didn't matter. I was going to eat it at the counter, then go back to work.

I had just taken my first bite when the doorbell rang.

I frowned and set my plate on the counter before going to check who it was.

My heart warmed and a huge smile spread over my face as I opened the door for Heath.

"Hey, I didn't know you were coming over."

He shrugged and looked past me.

"Sorry. Long day. Can I come in?"

There was something in his tone that worried me, but I stepped back and put my hand on his chest.

He didn't kiss me. He didn't touch me.

What was going on?

"I just made dinner but there's probably enough for two. If you're hungry."

He shook his head. "No, I'm fine. Thanks though. It smells good."

"It smells okay. I had a long day at work, but I'm trying to eat something that isn't junk food. Pasta counts, right?"

"Yeah. Sure."

I frowned, trying to read his face. "What's wrong? Did your parents come back?"

He snorted and stuffed his hands in his pockets. "No,

they're long gone. They said they would stay for a bit, but they left. There's nothing here for them. I think, hopefully, they're realizing that."

Something cold washed over me, at the frankness in his tone, the anger. I couldn't fix this. He had to do it. Or maybe he had to realize that there was nothing to fix.

"Why don't you take a seat? Can I get you something to drink?"

"I can't stay long, Devney."

Again, that sick feeling hit me, and I swallowed down the nausea.

"Okay," I said calmly, though there was nothing calm about me.

"So, yeah. I've just been thinking. And, you know, this has been great. The two of us. Really great."

I nodded, not sure I could actually speak.

"But, I don't know, after the other night, and the fact that I really haven't even been home alone much, I don't know, I think we should take some space."

Space. I couldn't even say the word. I couldn't say anything, there was a sense of foreboding and rage pushing inside me. My palms went sweaty. I was so fucking confused about what was happening. "You need to see the world and be with other people before you settle down. You fell into this with me. I was your lie. And now you need to find a truth, you know? Figure it out."

He was saying words but they didn't make sense. As if

he were trying to explain to himself what he was doing, and why he was making these decisions, and yet all I wanted to do was yell at him and ask what the hell he was doing and why he thought this was a good idea.

It felt as if the world was crumbling beneath me.

"Are you kidding me?" I asked, staring up at him.

"Devney, you deserve the world. You deserve someone who actually knows what the fuck he's doing."

"You don't know what you're doing right now, that is clear."

"Devney."

"Don't talk to me in that tone. You're breaking things off because you're scared? Because of your parents? You're not your father, and you're not your mother. You know that."

"You know where I come from. You have this huge family that cares about you, who are always up in your business because they love you. You deserve that. You deserve someone that's going to mesh with them. You don't need my fucked-up family."

"So, you're telling me your brothers and sister are fucked up?"

"Greer's finally found something, and hopefully it'll work, but my brothers? You don't know what Luca's been through, and it's not my place to say, and August? He was fucking married to your boss and we don't even talk about it. Of course, we're fucked up. I don't want to hurt you."

"Too fucking late."

His eyes widened at my use of profanity, since I didn't curse as much as he did.

"What? You're surprised that I'm fighting back? You're walking out on this because you're scared. Because you're afraid that you're what, going to fall in love with me and then we'll fall apart like your parents did? I am sorry for the shitty things they did. They are terrible parents that didn't deserve you. You guys would've been better off with the four of you alone, without them. I know that, and I hope you do too. But you are not them. Don't break this off because you're scared."

"Devney." He let out a deep breath. "There's nothing to break off. We were your practice run. Remember? I was your good time. The guy to stand in so you could have a moment to breathe and your family wouldn't set you up on dates. I did that. And you stood up to your family. So, you don't need me anymore."

"That's a lie," I whispered, tears streaming down my face. I hated that I was crying, I wanted to stop. He couldn't see this. I was fighting for him, but he wasn't fighting for me.

"I'm just going to hurt you. That's what we do."

And then he walked out, closing the door behind him. I just stared, wondering what the hell happened.

He wanted me to be with other people. He wanted me to find someone better than him.

Carrie Ann Ryan

Only, I had done the stupid thing. I believed in the lie. I had fallen for him.

And I was wrong. He might be scared, but if he loved me, he wouldn't have walked away.

I hadn't realized that being wrong could hurt so much.

I fell to my knees and cried, and just wanted to wake up from this nightmare.

220

Chapter 17

Devney

Somehow, I made it through work the next day. Paisley was in meetings all day, and I ignored texts from Addison. All I did was work, put on a bright smile, and hoped the concealer hid the dark shadows under my eyes.

I was just so tired of everything. I had been wrong. Everything hurt, and I couldn't fix it.

I had family dinner that night, and I couldn't get out of it. Not when I had thrown the bombshell I had before. Well, throwing another one tonight would be fun. My body ached, and all I wanted to do was go to sleep.

It turned out that Heath Cassidy was a first for many things. The first man I had made love to.

The first man I had fallen for.

And the first man that had broken my heart.

Go Heath.

I washed my face in cold water, trying to wake myself up. I had to do this family thing, then I could go home and hide under the covers. Then I could figure out how to be strong again. Because I had fought back. I'd fought for myself. I lost, but I had fought. So this crying jag just needed to go away.

The doorbell rang and I stiffened. It wouldn't be him. He wasn't coming back. He had made that clear. I didn't want to talk to anyone, but when someone started pounding on the door, and a familiar voice yelled through it, I knew who it was.

It wasn't my family; they didn't know. They had no idea that he'd broken my heart.

But apparently I hadn't been able to hide the tears at work after all.

I opened the door to see Paisley and Addison standing there. Addison with fire in her eyes, Paisley with a sense of understanding in hers.

"Why didn't you tell me?" Addison asked as she stormed in and threw her arms around me. I let her hold me as I looked over her shoulder at Paisley.

Paisley shrugged. "You didn't have to say anything. I saw it on your face this morning. I knew we were both busy, so I tried to let you be. But then you didn't tell Addison. So I decided to intervene. Tell us what happened."

Addison let me go but took my hand and pulled me into the living room.

"He broke it off. I don't really know what more to say."

"It doesn't make any sense. He loves you. Anyone could see that."

I snorted, but it was more like a rough chuckle with a sob in the middle.

"I don't think that's true."

"He did. I saw the way he looked at you," Addison said softly. "There's no way someone could look at you like that and not love you."

"But he broke it off."

I looked at Paisley, who still wasn't saying anything, and explained about the dinner.

"His parents sound like royal pains in the asses. Abusive and horrible."

"I agree. Horrible, horrible people. But he can't see past that. He sees them and somehow thinks he's going to do the same thing. It doesn't make any sense. Because he has tried so hard to cultivate a relationship with his family, and then as soon as things got hard, as soon as his family reminded him of how he'd grown up, he went back. It doesn't make any sense to me."

"It breaks your heart to lose a Cassidy brother."

I looked at Paisley as she spoke, her gaze distant. I didn't know what she was seeing, but it wasn't me.

223

Carrie Ann Ryan

"They are wonderful men. Greer is an amazing woman. They fight so hard for each other, but they forget to fight for themselves. Because as soon as their parents find a way to needle back into their lives, it's like a switch hits. And they can't get through it. It doesn't matter what logic says. It doesn't matter if they think they're above it. All they see is who they were and what they could be. Not what they are. And there's no changing that."

"So, just like that, he gives up. He doesn't fight."

"He's too busy fighting himself."

I shook my head, disgusted. "It doesn't make any sense. Why would he do that?"

"Because in his mind he doesn't have a choice. It's stupid and I hate it, and I hate their parents for doing that to them. I don't know exactly what went on with their parents. I know there was cheating, mental and physical abuse on both sides. There's so much more. They never hit their kids, but they forgot to love them along the way. They're just pawns for each other. And that broke something inside those boys. Inside Greer. She's figuring it out because she's finally leaning on the men she loves. But the guys? I don't know about Luca, it's not like August really let me get to know them when we were married." She sounded as hollow as I felt.

"I don't understand. I don't understand why this happens. Why we do this."

"I just want to go and kick his ass. To kick Luca's too. Because he didn't tell me," Addison said into the quiet.

"He didn't tell you about what?" I asked.

"He didn't tell me about you and Heath."

"I don't think Heath would tell them. He wouldn't want to put any more pressure on them because he's the big brother."

"I hate this. I hate this so much. I don't know how to fix it."

"Then we kick his ass," Addison suggested.

"Or maybe we don't fix it. Maybe we just watch the Cassidy brothers destroy themselves because they're really good at destroying us."

With that ominous statement from Paisley, we sat in silence for a while, before Addison pulled out some cheese from the refrigerator and made me eat a little before I realized I needed to leave for my parents' house.

By the time they left, I was running late, but it didn't matter. I just needed to get there and find a way through. Heath didn't love me. If he had, he wouldn't have pushed me away. I needed to realize that. He was just my first boyfriend.

There was an accident on 70, so I followed traffic towards C470, taking the long way towards the darkening mountains and the setting sun and my parents' house.

I was exhausted, and I just wanted to get this over

with. To make sure that Maureen and the others knew I loved them and that I was sorry for lying.

And then tell them the lie wasn't quite a lie anymore. Because Heath wasn't mine.

Love hurt, men sucked, and I was exhausted.

I was going the speed limit, taking the middle lane as I passed a few people going slower than traffic, when the car in front of me did a weird movement. I gripped the steering wheel, holding back a scream as everything seemed to go in slow motion. The Jeep in front of me hit something dark in the middle of the road, and flipped over on its top and skidded, sparks flying everywhere. I jerked the wheel, doing the one thing I knew I shouldn't, and then I was spinning out on the highway. Thankfully there wasn't a car next to me. I spun once, twice, and again, and then I skidded off the side of the highway; as the car hit the grass, I flipped. I screamed as the airbags exploded, the sound of crunching metals reached my ears, and then there was nothing.

Chapter 18

Heath

"Okay what crawled up your ass and died, other than the lovely surprise we had a few days ago," August asked, and I shrugged, looking back to the instructions. We were trying to build a bookshelf for Luca's office, and as the instructions were in Spanish, I was trying to remember what each word meant. I could have pulled out my phone and used a translation app, but why would I bother doing that? Doing things in the most complicated way possible and wanting to slam my head against the partially erected bookshelf was much easier.

"Well, I got a text from Addison yelling at me, so I think I know what happened," Luca said, looking at another set of instructions for the table he was putting together.

We loved this furniture place, but for some reason they hadn't sent the right instructions, and now we were taking far too long to figure out how to build the pieces we'd bought. It should have been intuitive, but honestly, nothing made sense.

Just like in life.

"Did you break up with Devney?" Greer asked, and I turned to look at my sister who was helping Luca.

"What?"

"He did," Luca answered with a growl.

"What the hell? Stop talking about me behind my back."

"Right now, we're talking about you in front of you," August snapped. "What the hell were you thinking? Devney's the best thing that's ever happened to you."

"So says the man who got married and divorced and didn't really tell us anything about it." I could have cut off my own tongue, because I never wanted to hurt my brother like that, and from the flash in August's eyes, the barb hit the mark.

"Stop, just stop it," Luca snapped. "Why are we fighting? This isn't us."

"No, it's our lovely parents," Greer replied.

She threw up her hands and we all stared at her. "What? Why are you surprised I said that? We're trying to be better at being siblings. You guys moved out here to be near me and start over. And I love you for it. But we don't talk about the fact that our parents suck. They left us. Sure, I had Mom and you had Dad, but what did that mean? They were too busy squabbling with each other and trying to hurt one another using us, that we got thrown into the fire. I love you guys. I love getting to know you. But I missed all those years, just like you did with me. I'm trying to be open about my relationship with you guys. You know Noah and Ford and call them friends and I love it. But I never even met Paisley when you were married, August. I don't know why you got married or why you got divorced. And if you're not ready to say anything about that to us? Then maybe you should talk to somebody. But I'd love to hear. And Luca, you never talk about Ashleigh."

Luca flinched. "I know. I should. I just don't know what there is to say about Ashleigh. We loved each other. She was my best friend. And she died. Now I'm here. You met her though. You got to know her at least a little."

I rubbed my hand over my heart as Luca spoke about Ashleigh for the first time in what felt like months. He never mentioned her. She was the reason for most of his decisions when he was younger, the reason for the path he chose. The reason he hated our parents. And the reason he lived here.

And there was nothing I could do as a big brother to help him. To protect him. Just like I hadn't been able to protect Greer or August.

"Don't get that look on your face," Luca snapped. "You're my big brother, I get it. But you do not have to solve all of our problems. You couldn't have saved my girlfriend. Nobody could. And yes, it took me a while to fucking figure that out on my own. I couldn't save Ashleigh. Apparently August and Paisley weren't right for each other, but Greer's happy. She's so damn happy." He grinned over at Greer, who just snorted and shook her head. "But you? Why did you push Devney away?"

I threw my hands up in the air. "Because I'm just going to hurt her. Did you not hear what you all just said? What our parents did? They constantly cheat on each other and hit each other and use us as pawns. They were going to do the same to her."

"Then you protect her," August said, so softly, it was barely above a whisper.

"I'll just hurt her."

"You did hurt her," Luca said. "Why do you think that you can't move on from what our parents did? Why do you think that you can't have a relationship?"

"I would like to know that, too. Because I have a relationship with two men I love. I'm going to marry them. We're going to raise a family. You can do it, too. Do you just not love her?"

"She's everything," I ground out.

"Then why?" August asked. "I know why Paisley and I didn't work out. And it doesn't have anything to do with what you think." He held up his hands. "I can't talk about it. It's not my place. Just know that I will hate our parents until the end of my days. They hurt us and they hurt who we love. But they don't matter. They're nothing. If I never saw them again, it would be too soon. But *we* matter. The four of us in this room. You have always taken on the mantle of big brother. Always wanted to protect us. But protect yourself. We're not going to have the same problems our parents did. Fix it. We know you love her. Take a chance."

I ran my hand over my heart as I looked at my siblings, the people I would do anything for, and realized I was a fucking idiot.

"But what if I make a mistake? What if I hurt her?"

"Then fix it and say you're sorry and mean it. Life isn't perfect. Relationships aren't perfect. They take a lot of work and a lot of communication, but you can make it work. You just have to try and commit."

August's phone rang, interrupting the moment, and he frowned, looking down at the readout. "Why is Paisley calling me?" he asked.

"Answer it. If she's calling you, it's for a reason."

August nodded at Greer's words and answered.

"Paisley? What's wrong?"

The phone was loud enough that I could hear the other end, and my blood turned to ice. "Don't speak. I can't. I can't think. But it's Devney. She's hurt. I don't know how bad, but please come to the hospital. Addison's on her way, too. But just please come. Bring the family."

"Paisley?" August asked.

"She'll need him." And then she hung up. I was running towards my car, my family on my heels. Luca grabbed the keys out of my hand and pushed me towards the passenger door.

"You're shaking. It's my turn."

"Get us there. Just get us there."

"I'll get you there."

Greer was on the phone, talking to her men, while August leaned forward from behind me and gripped my shoulder.

"She didn't say what kind of accident?" I asked, my hands shaking.

"No," August said. "You heard the whole conversation. She just said the hospital." August named it again and I nodded. Luca drove quickly, but safely. My hands shook so I was grateful he was there.

"She has to be okay. She has to be."

"She will be." I looked back at Greer, who met my gaze. "She will be. And you're going to grovel and say you love her, and everything's going to be fine. Do you want the guys there?"

"If you need them. But if her family's there, that might be too many people."

"Okay. We're here for you. She'll have you, but you'll have us. Remember that. You'll always have us."

I swallowed the knot of emotion in my throat as Luca pulled into the ER. We piled out and ran in. I didn't need to ask the nurse up front where Devney was, because I could see her family. All of them. The stepsiblings, the half-siblings, her parents. The spouses and kids weren't there, but it was a big enough group anyway.

Devney's mother met my gaze and walked over. From the look of compassion and fear in her eyes, she and the others didn't know that I had broken her baby girl's heart. That I didn't have a right to be there.

"Oh, I'm glad you're here. We realized that none of us had your number, but Paisley knew how to contact you." She gestured towards Paisley, who was walking towards the front door while Addison ran through.

"Any news? What's going on?" Addison glared and pushed past me. "What are you doing here?" Addison asked.

Luca pulled her off. "Be quiet."

She glared at him but didn't say anything else.

"She's in the back, I don't know what's going on. We're still waiting to hear. There was an accident. A huge truck dropped four or five mattresses on the highway in the dark, and cars hit them. Devney overcorrected when she was trying to get out of the way of the Jeep that flipped in front of her, and she spun out. She was lucky she didn't hit another car when she did 360s on the highway, but flipped when she hit the embankment. The airbags went off, and people stopped to help her. But I don't know any more than that. They got her in an ambulance and brought her here."

I opened my arms, the only thing I could do, and she sank into me, crying into my chest. Devney's father held one of his daughters, as my family mingled with Devney's, and we waited for news.

It felt like hours.

Waiting to hear if the woman I loved was alive, if she would be okay.

She had to be.

Because I never told her I loved her. I had hurt her, and I needed to fix it.

I needed her to know I was coming for her before this accident. Before I thought I could lose her forever. Because I couldn't. I couldn't bear the thought.

I hated that it had taken me this long to realize that.

"Womack family?"

We all stood, all of us, and the doctor's eyes widened, before finding Devney's parents.

"We're all family," Devney's mother said as she gripped Addison's hand. I stood behind them, my hands shaking. Luca and Greer stood on either side of me, August behind me with his hand on my shoulder.

"Your daughter will be fine. She needed surgery to

repair some things." He listed them, but I couldn't hear anything after "she will be fine."

But she had been hurt. She'd needed surgery.

And I hadn't been there. Hadn't been there to protect her.

"She'll be in recovery soon, but we can't let all of you back there at once."

"Can I see her? Can we see our daughter?" Devney's stepfather asked.

"Soon. Once she's awake from the anesthesia. Most of you can go home, though. It's late, almost past visiting hours."

"We'll wait to hear," Maureen said, her chin raised. "We'll stake out this corner and stay out of the way. But we'll wait to talk to our sister."

The man nodded and left. I finally staggered back to a seat. August helped me sit down, and I put my hands over my face, letting the tears come.

I nearly lost her. Nearly lost her when I didn't even have her.

I would fix this. I would fix us.

But first, I needed to make sure she was okay.

Chapter 19
Devney

Everything ached. It felt as if I had been put through the wringer, or perhaps flipped in a car.

But I was alive. At least that's what my doctors told me.

"A broken arm, bruised ribs, bruises all over your body, and a slight concussion. But you're here. My baby's here." My mom leaned forward and kissed my cheeks.

"You worried us so much."

"I think I worried myself as well."

"But you're okay," Maureen said from my side.

It was just the three of them: my stepfather, my mother, and Maureen. The other siblings said they would be in tomorrow. I knew I would have to see them all, and I

237

wanted to. I wanted to see everyone. And I also just wanted to sleep.

"They received hell this morning, and we kicked out most of the family so they could get some sleep as well and we wouldn't take over the whole waiting room."

My stepdad snorted. "I'm pretty sure they were going to call security on all of us. Plus, your friends were there too, and we took over three-quarters of the place just being here."

I smiled and ignored the slight ache from the cut on my lip. My window had shattered, and I had cuts on my chest and arms. My face was bruised from the airbags, and my arm was broken. but other than that, I would be okay.

At least, they kept saying it.

I had broken my ulna, which was going to suck to heal, because I already had ulna nerve issues from typing so much, but I would get back to work. I would be fine. I hadn't broken anything else.

I was just sore.

"I'm so sorry," I blurted, and my mom frowned. "It wasn't your fault. It was that truck's fault. I'm so mad that they dropped those mattresses and didn't even notice. They didn't even come back. I am just relieved you're going to be okay. The people from the Jeep in front of you are going to be okay as well, though I think they have a longer healing journey from what I can put together by speaking with their families."

That made me smile again, tugging at the cut on my lip.

"Of course, you're talking to the other families."

"Why wouldn't I? I wanted to make sure they were okay too. You're going to come home with us and we're going to take care of you. I can't believe we almost lost you." My mom blinked back tears as my stepdad wrapped his arm around her shoulders. "Now, stop that. Every time that you make your daughter frown or laugh it hurts her lip. Let's be good, okay?"

"I'm sorry. I'm sorry. I'm fine. And you're fine. We're all fine."

"I don't think she's sorry about the accident," Maureen sat up, studying my face. "I think she's still sorry about the whole Heath thing."

I met her gaze, and though we weren't blood-related, it was as if we were connected on every level. She was my sister. She had been my big sister since I was a little girl, and she loved me. Cared for me. Was always there. Even when it was almost too much.

"Why are you still worried about that?" my mom asked.

"I'm just so sorry. For lying."

"That doesn't matter anymore," my mom said, so fiercely that I knew if anyone argued with her, she would probably punch them.

"Mom's right," Maureen put in. "We're pushy. All of

us. In fact, I sort of pushed the family into making me the head person to speak about the fact that we're so sorry for being pushy."

I wanted to shake my head at that, but I would just hurt myself with the minor concussion.

"We're so sorry for being pushy when we think we know what's best for you. Clearly, you could always make your own decisions. We just want you to be happy. And we sometimes forget that we are like the wolves from that Hotel Transylvania thing and we sort of run around in a pack and take over."

"I do the same things when it comes to making sure you guys are okay, though. And making sure the younger kids are fine."

"Because we're family."

"We are. I love you all so much. And I know sometimes I feel like I stand in my own way being the perpetual middle child, but I do love you. And I promise I'll do better."

"You're my child," my stepdad said so fiercely that my eyes widened. "I was so blessed to find your mother." He gripped my mother's hand and squeezed. "I had a beautiful wife and five beautiful children, and then I was all alone until I found your mom. She is the best thing that ever happened to us. She immediately became their mother, and I did my best to be your father."

"I'm sorry I didn't always let you."

"I never met the man who raised you, but I'm blessed he had you. Because you are a light for all of us. He is part of this family, even if he didn't get to meet us all."

Now I was freely crying, and he leaned forward and wiped my tears.

"You are a wonderful human being. And you're my daughter. I love you, Devney. Never scare me like that again. You understand that? You don't get to scare me like this."

"I'll do my best, Dad." I whispered.

His eyes warmed, Maureen sniffed, and my mother patted Maureen's shoulders.

Because he had always been my stepfather, or William. He had never really been Dad. That was on me because I hadn't wanted to forget my father. But I wouldn't. I needed to remember that. Because I had that base, a base that Heath never had. But one he was gaining, at least I thought.

Why on earth was I thinking about him?

I was so tired, and I knew they would leave me alone soon so I could go back to sleep, but then my stepdad cleared his throat. "There also seems to be someone else waiting for you. Just know I'll protect you no matter what."

And with that ominous statement, they left, hugging me and saying they loved me, then suddenly Heath was there.

I didn't know who had called him, but I knew that someone would have. I knew my friends would be here any minute too, because that's who we were. We were a unit.

Just like I thought Heath and I had been.

"Devney."

"Hey."

Not the most eloquent thing to say, but I wasn't sure what else there was. "I'd get up to say hello, but I'm really tired."

"I won't stay long." Again, that hurt slapped at me but I ignored it. "I know you need your rest. But I've been here all night with your family, and I was so fucking scared I might lose you."

"Heath," I began, and swallowed hard. But he had lost me. He'd pushed me away, hadn't he?

"I'm so sorry for pushing you away. I was talking to my family right before we heard about the accident, and I was trying to figure out how to grovel. How to come back and tell you I'm sorry and I shouldn't have left, that I was standing in my own way. I didn't know how to fix it. And then Paisley called."

I sat up so quickly that I hurt my ribs. Heath was suddenly there, gripping my hand.

"No, sit back. Don't hurt yourself."

"Sorry," I said through gritted teeth. "Paisley called?" I asked.

"She called August," he said dryly.

My eyes widened. "Oh my God."

"Pretty much."

We both smiled, that shared connection pulling us, even though I was scared he was going to walk away again. I didn't know what I was supposed to do or what I was supposed to say. I had never been in this situation before. I didn't have answers. I didn't know if there were any.

"Devney. I'm so sorry. I got scared. I saw who my parents were, realized the loop they were in, and it just blinded me. It always has. It's why I cling so hard to my family now and I feel like I can't protect my sister. That's why I feel like I'm constantly failing all of them. And I know that's on me, and I need to get over it, and I'm working on it. Or, at least I thought I was. But then I realized that I fucking love you and I was so afraid that love was going to twist into something like theirs that I pushed you away."

I held up my hand. "Did you just say you loved me?" I asked, the words coming out slowly as I tried to figure out what the hell was going on.

"I do." He stood back and pushed his hand through his long hair. "I love you so damn much, it scares me. When you came into the bar the first night, I knew there was something special about you, but then I didn't get your number, and I never saw you again until you were there, hands out, trying to ward off your family. I think I fell partly in love with you that night."

"You have to be joking."

"No, I'm serious. And I kept telling myself that I was just here to show you around, to teach you about dating. I'd be the perfect fake boyfriend that was partially real. But it was all just so I wouldn't freak out. And I know that is a dumbass thing to say and it's weak, but I'm trying to do better. I'm never going to do that again. I promise. I can't lose you."

"You weren't going to lose me. Until you pushed me away. It hurt, Heath. And I don't want to ever feel that again."

"I promise. We're going to talk it out, and I'm going to act like the fucking adult that I am. I promise I'll never do that again."

"I didn't want to fall for you," I said after a moment.

His eyes widened and he swallowed hard. "I didn't want to fall for you, either."

"But I did fall. I love you. And you've seen my family, you see the way that I'm trying to not push them away. I get it. So I guess we're going to have to do better together."

He pushed my hair from my face, so gentle the ache was real. "We can figure out families together. Because we have a really big family, Devney. Both of us. And they want what's best for us. At least, the family that counts."

"So, you're not going to run away?"

"Never. I almost lost you twice, once from my stupid decisions, and the other from an accident. I never want to lose you. And I never want you to think that you're going to lose me."

He leaned down and gently brushed his lips against the side of my mouth, away from the cut.

"You were the perfect imaginary boyfriend, you know."

"Yeah?" he asked, laughter in his gaze.

"But I think I like you better a little rough. A little wrong. You make silly decisions, just like I do."

"So, let's do better."

"Together?" I asked.

"Together. And I promise I'll grovel a bit more when you're out of this hospital bed."

"Good. I've always wanted to see a boyfriend grovel."

"I guess I'll be your first." A kiss. "And your only."

I sighed into him.

He was right.

My only.

Chapter 20

Heath

Light slanted through the blinds and danced over her skin. The sheet had pulled down below to her thighs, uncovering the rest of her. She slept well, and after everything that had happened, I was glad she was sleeping.

Though I had kept her up the night before, we had kept each other up. So perhaps that was also my fault.

But it was all I could do not to reach out and gently trail my finger over her breasts. They were full, her nipples hard. She still slept, but her body ached. Fuck, so did mine.

I played with her nipples, loving the way that she arched for me. She was slowly waking up, but I wanted to wake her up myself. So I trailed my fingers down her stomach, her hips, and over her mound. I cupped her, loving the way that she groaned into me.

"That's my girl. Lean into my touch."

She was hot between her legs, dampening my hand.

It was hard to breathe when she was in the room, but it didn't matter. All that mattered was that I wanted her, and she wanted me.

"Heath," she whispered, her eyes fluttering open.

"There's my girl."

She smiled softly. "There's my boyfriend," she teased.

I chuckled, the sound rusty. There hadn't been much laughing when I was so fucking scared that I would lose her. And not just from the accident, but from my own stupidity.

She must have read my thoughts, because she looked up at me and cupped my face. My beard was rough against her palm, and I knew I should shave. Especially with how I wanted to touch her. But I couldn't move, not when she looked at me like that.

"We're safe, Heath."

"Are we, girlfriend?" I asked, teasing.

"Yes, boyfriend. We're safe. I love you."

"I love you, too. But I'm never going to get the look of you in that hospital bed out of my mind."

"But I'm safe. So kiss me, make love to me. And then we'll deal with everything else."

"Well, since you asked so sweetly."

I smiled, then took her lips with mine.

My fingers delved between her folds, needing to touch her, wanting her. I slowly, oh so slowly pressed a finger deep inside her. She arched in the bed, achingly soft, achingly sweet.

"That's my girl."

"Heath," she murmured before she reached down and took me in hand.

I groaned, practically bucking into her hold. But I kept steady and didn't come right there.

It was damn hard. Not with that perfect touch of hers. But I would hold on, because I had to. Because if I didn't, I wouldn't have her coming around me. And I needed to feel that sweet cunt around my cock.

I quickly counted to ten and reminded myself that I could hold on a bit longer.

We explored each other gently, my thumb over her clit as we kissed, touched, trying to send each other over the edge. And when her mouth parted against mine, a quiet gasp escaping, I smiled and felt her come over my hand.

"Oh my God," she mumbled, the phrase sounding like one word.

I kept playing with her, sliding my fingers over her, and then down between her cheeks, pressing my finger against her ass. Just to tease. We would be gentle, because

I would always be gentle with her, even when we went a bit harder.

We moved, and I settled between her thighs. Her legs cradled me, as if I was always meant to be there.

"You're so fucking beautiful."

"Funny. I was going to say the same about you."

"I love you," I whispered against her mouth.

She smiled up at me. "I love you, too. Always."

I entered her with a soft stroke, and then a harder one. She met me thrust for thrust. She was so tight, so hot, so wet, it was all I could do not to pound into her. But I held back, only because I knew she wanted us to take our time. She wanted to set the pace, though I was the one who usually thought I was in control. No, it was always Devney. Always my Devney.

When she came again, shouting my name this time, I rolled to my back and let her ride me, let her arch over me as her breasts bounced.

We kept moving, kept touching and kissing. And then we shifted again, this time with her on her knees, hand on the wall, as I pounded into her from behind. My fingers found her clit, the moves a little rougher, a little more aggressive. A little more everything.

"Play with your breasts."

"I'll fall," she said, her hands holding onto the wall for dear life.

"I'll catch you," I whispered as I sucked on her neck, then bit down on her shoulder.

She nodded, her whole body shaking, before she moved one hand off the wall and played with her breasts, rolling her nipples between her fingers.

"That's my girl."

I continued to move until there was nothing else I could do—I came with her next orgasm. When we both fell into a pile of limbs and sweat and need, I looked at her and smiled.

"Damn," I whispered.

"That's one word for it," she said.

I took her lips again, needing her. I continued to move with soft, quick strokes. I was still hard. The woman constantly did that to me.

I kept moving, just needing to hold her. Needing to touch her.

"Be with me. Move in with me."

I hadn't meant to say the words then. I wanted to go slow. To figure out who we were.

But I really couldn't help myself.

She lay cradled in my arms and smiled up at me.

"I was already going to take over a few drawers and just not tell you."

I laughed and shook my head. "Really? Starting it off like that?"

"Well, you started off as my imaginary boyfriend, then

my fake one. I might as well make me your live-in girl-friend. Even without asking."

I took her mouth in a greedy kiss, and then smiled.

"Sounds like a plan."

"You really were the best imaginary boyfriend."

"Well, seems like I have a lot to live up to."

"I think you're doing a pretty good job."

"Good. I'm never letting you go."

"You think you have a choice? I was never going to let you."

We laughed and held on to one another. We made love again, and I had a feeling we would be late to family dinner.

But honestly, I didn't care. Not with the woman that I loved in my arms.

And a promise of forever I hadn't planned.

Chapter 21

Devney

The noise in the house had now reached a level I wasn't sure would ever quiet down. People talked in loud voices to speak over one another, raising their octaves as they laughed or wanted to tell a story. They spoke over one another, interrupted one another, and then paused to listen.

Nobody was fighting, nobody was pushing or arguing or threatening. They just looked happy, and as if this all made sense and they had done it countless times before.

Heath and I stood in the back, wide-eyed, wondering what exactly was happening.

"Did you invite them all?" I asked, trying to speak low so my voice wouldn't carry.

"I mentioned to my family that we should have family

dinner, but I didn't know that this was what they meant by family dinner."

"It wasn't me," I said, and then another voice spoke up.

"And it also wasn't me," Addison said as she came to hide behind us.

"Wait, did I know you were here?" I asked, before I hugged her. "Why are you hiding? You know everybody here."

"But there's so many of them. I'm really outnumbered."

Heath snorted beside me.

"You think you're outnumbered. The Cassidys aren't even close to being the dominant predators here."

Addison and I both burst out laughing.

"Predators?"

"You heard me," Heath mumbled, but then everyone seemed to turn towards us.

"You're here!" my mom yelled, before Alice Womack Johnson came over and hugged me.

Before I could respond, she did the same to Heath while my stepfather hugged me, and then each one of my siblings came at me. Everyone continued to talk while the step-sibs hugged us, then the half-sibs moved in as one, as if they were a group of rabid wolves from the movie *Hotel Transylvania*.

I'd always been worried that I hadn't fit in. That I'd

been the one kid without the same mom or the same dad and without the same name. But they had always loved me. They always counted me as their own.

When I was hurt, they dropped everything and came to me. They had organized childcare and made sure the spouses were all ready to do anything needed so our family was safe. And it was the same with the Cassidys.

It was the Johnsons, Cassidys, Womacks, and everyone we counted as family.

I had kept my name to honor my father, but perhaps part of me had also kept it to set myself apart, because I was so afraid they would leave, just like my dad had. Even though he hadn't had a choice.

But you couldn't stop the brain of a little girl who was so sad and afraid.

I loved my family. I loved their robustness, how loud they were.

And I loved how easily they took in the Cassidys as if they were their own.

My mother and stepfather already decided that Heath and his siblings were theirs. It didn't matter that Heath and I weren't married, that we were only dating. That he had been my fake and imaginary boyfriend before this.

No, my mother would mother them, and Heath and his family had no say in it.

"Why are you crying?" my mom asked as she wiped my tears.

Heath had been absorbed into the horde of siblings, and I knew I had to go save him. Eventually.

"I was just thinking how much I love you guys."

My mother let out a soft gasp before she pulled me closer. "I love you so much, daughter of mine. And both of your dads do, too."

William cleared his throat as he pulled us into his arms. "You're my daughter. And I'll be forever grateful that Hunter gave me you."

"And there goes that," I said, tears flowing down my face.

Somehow Heath extracted himself from my youngest sibling and came over to me. "Are you okay? What is it? Are you hurting?"

"I'm fine. I'm just happy."

He looked perplexed, but my mother just waved him off. "It's a woman thing."

"I don't know, I cry when I'm happy too," August said, with such a deadpan voice I burst out laughing.

"You guys are ridiculous, and I love you all. I still can't believe we all fit into this house."

We were in my parents' house, and I was amazed they had seating for everyone. Barely.

"Well, some of us may be eating on the floor at the coffee table, but that's fine. The kiddie table may also be in the laundry room."

"My family and I are grateful that you invited us," Heath said, as he wrapped his arm around my shoulders.

"Well, as Luca is already sampling the veggie trays as he talks to the children, I have a feeling we're going to be one big, blended family soon."

I stiffened, as Heath cleared his throat. "Thank you. We're still getting used to this whole family thing. I kind of like it."

I was grateful that Heath had taken it like that, and not the whole marriage and family and name thing. Because Heath and I were still learning how we loved each other. How we blended.

I wasn't ready to be married. To have a horde of children like my stepsiblings. But I was ready to live with and spend my life with Heath.

One day at a time.

Somehow, we found a place to eat, sitting between Luca and one of my brothers. August had been conscripted to go sit with the younger siblings, and I just laughed, loving the way everybody seemed to get along, even though we were all different people with our own stories.

When dessert came out, I was so full I knew I would burst soon.

But I had almost lost everything, and didn't even realize I had it all to begin with. I could still see the lights flashing, headlights then darkness, headlights then darkness.

But I had survived.

"Are you okay?" Heath asked, his voice low beneath the din of conversations around us.

"I'm wonderful."

"I love you, fake girlfriend," he whispered.

"I love you, imaginary boyfriend."

Luca made a choking sound, and I narrowed my gaze at him, before he grinned and turned to joke with Addison.

We were all family. In a complicated sort of way. And I was so damn happy.

I hadn't meant to be. Hadn't thought this was in my future.

But it was.

I was a daughter, a sister, an aunt, a friend, and a girl-friend. I would take those labels any day, and any more that came at me. Because I could stand up for myself, I could love, I could fear, and I could breathe. And I would never do it alone. Because I had my family, and I had Heath.

The most unexpected present of all.

Chapter 22

Addison

I was not a fan of waiting. It broke time into measurements that either slowed down or sped up, depending on what you waited for. And I was not good at waiting.

I wanted to know, needed to know what would happen once I finished this.

But that meant I would have to wait for it.

"Addison?"

I turned to see Luca standing there, my best friend. Well, one of them. Somehow, when the world hadn't been watching, Luca Cassidy had become my best friend.

Devney was my childhood best friend and would always be like a sister. Paisley was quickly becoming a best friend.

But there was one thing I learned growing up, that

those words mattered and changed over time. That I could have more than one best friend. Each person in my life meant something different to me.

Luca and I had clicked the moment we met. I would be forever grateful that Devney had faked a relationship with his brother.

"What?" I asked when he said something else. I was lost in my own thoughts, trying to figure out what was going on.

Because honestly this all felt like a dream.

"I asked if you needed something to drink. You know. To help."

I snorted, because he looked just as lost as I did.

"I'm really not good at this, Luca."

"You too? Because this is a first for me. And I'm not good at firsts."

"Oh, I'm pretty sure you're good at firsts," I joked before I sat down on the bar stool next to me and put my hands over my face and screamed.

Luca was there in an instant. His hands on my shoulders as he kept me steady.

That was Luca, the steady one.

I pretended to be steady. I freaked out and screamed and pretended I knew what I was doing.

But in the end, I didn't. I had no idea what to do or how to fix it.

"Do you want to go for a walk? Do you want me to

feed you? Please just tell me what to do right now."

I lowered my hands and looked up at my best friend. "I have no idea what to do either. This is really poor timing."

"Well, I think it's the timing that needed to happen."

I blinked. "Are you just trying to spout off sage crap that makes no sense but sounds good so you feel better and in control of the situation?"

Luca nodded. "Of course. It's how I work with cats who really don't want anything to do with me. I talk calmly, and then my staff and I tackle the poor thing and hide its little head so it's not scared anymore."

I blinked, trying to figure out where he was going with this. "Are you saying I'm an uncontrollable cat with a biting issue?"

Luca smirked, his eyes going dark and smokey. "Oh, I know you like biting."

I froze for a minute before I snorted and laughed, flipping him off. It was exactly the reaction he wanted because I knew he was trying to relax both of us.

"So. Seen any good movies lately?" he asked.

"You know I've been working eighty-hour weeks, and I don't actually know what movies are anymore."

Luca sat next to me, his hand on mine, as we waited. And waited.

"You work longer hours than I do, and I don't get any time off."

He gestured toward the sleeping elderly collie mix currently on my couch. When Luca had shown up right after I texted him saying it was an emergency, he had the elderly dog with him. I normally wasn't a pet-on-furniture type of person, but I had seen those wide eyes, and not just Luca's, and known that Reginald the Fifth needed time to have anything he wanted.

"I hate that his owners aren't here anymore and now Reginald doesn't have any family but us."

"I'm not good at family, Luca. I'm good at working, and fighting for what I need. I'm really not good at this."

"You can be. And we both know Reginald's sick. We'll take care of him for his last days so he won't be alone."

I blinked tears away. "It's not fair. And they don't get as much time as we do."

"As is evidenced by Reginald's parents, time is short for everyone. And we have to live it through. Reginald's happy right now. He has people who love him and make sure he's comfy. And he's sleeping on your precious, precious couch that you don't even let me sit on."

"That was one time, and you were sweaty from a run. You could have sat in that chair, but no, you wanted to sprawl all over my new couch."

"And tonight you put sheets on your couch so Reginald would be comfortable. You're a good woman, Addison. That's why you're my friend."

He squeezed my hand, before my phone buzzed.

We both looked down at the alarm, tension riding us.

No, this wasn't true. Totally not happening.

But time didn't lie, it sneered at you, and kicked you in the ass. But it didn't lie.

I walked into the bathroom, Luca right on my heels, and we looked down.

And saw my world change.

Everything changed.

"Well, fuck," Luca murmured, bringing me out of the screaming inside my head that wouldn't stop.

The little window in front clearly said it all.

Pregnant.

I was pregnant.

Single.

Working eighty hours a week in a job that I loved with people that I hated. A job where being a woman was more than a mark against you, it was something you had to overcome.

And now I was gestating.

I was single. Alone, standing next to my best friend.

And pregnant.

This day couldn't possibly get any worse.

And with that thought, I whirled to the toilet and emptied my stomach—my best friend holding back my hair, and the father of my unborn baby as pale as I was.

Bonus Epilogue

Heath

"Good girl."

She smiled up at me, before hollowing her cheeks. When my dick pressed against the back of her throat, she hummed along me and I groaned, tugging at her hair.

"You don't want me to come right now, do you?"

In answer, she dug her fingernails into my thighs and continued to bob up and down, swallowing me whole.

In the years we had been together, we'd learned each other's moves, each other's emotions. It was all I could do not to push her back, put her knees up to her shoulders, and fuck her hard. But she wanted to taste me, wanted this moment that we had stolen from the rest of the world, so she set the pace.

"Good girl. That's a good girl."

She continued to bob her head, laughing at me when she pulled away. When she cupped my balls, and then moved her other hand around, spreading my cheeks to play with my ass, I groaned and tugged on her hair a little forcibly.

"Okay, girl, I'm not about to come down that pretty throat or on those breasts of yours. I want to be inside you."

"When was the last time I swallowed or spit?" she asked, and I clicked my tongue.

"Didn't you used to be the innocent virgin? When did you get such a dirty mouth?"

I tugged her up again, palming her breasts as she continued to use her hand on me.

"I might have been a virgin, but there was never anything innocent about me. I've always liked sucking your cock."

I slid my fingers between her folds, her wet honey sliding over my skin. "No, nothing innocent about you. I love your taste." I speared her with two fingers before pulling them out and slid my fingers into my mouth. I sucked them clean, then used my wet fingers over her lips. I forced them into her mouth, fucking her mouth with my fingers.

"Now, where were we?" I reached down, grabbed her by her thighs, and carried her to the bed.

She latched her mouth to mine, and I moved one hand to the back of her neck, controlling the angle. When I tossed her on the bed, she laughed, kicking her feet out. I covered her, needing her taste, just needing her.

Needed my wife.

I played with her breasts, then kissed down her stomach, over her mound, before spreading her before me and feasting. I loved this taste, I knew this taste. This was my wife, my everything.

It didn't seem real that this was mine, that *she* was mine. But no matter what we went through, I had her.

Just like she had me. What more did I need?

I continued to taste, to suck, to need. When she came on my face, my beard rough against her inner thighs, I didn't stop.

She tugged on my hair, growling. "We are almost out of time, and if you are not inside me in the next two seconds, I'm going to pout. And you hate when I pout."

I licked my lips, swallowing her taste. "I actually don't mind the pouting."

"Heath Cassidy."

I laughed and crawled up her, kissing her hard. Then I sat back, gripped her thighs, and plunged into her.

She let out a shout, her body quaking as she came just from the penetration. She was so beautiful when she came, sweet and flushed and pulsing over my cock. It was all I could do not to come just from that. But I held back and held on. She gripped the bedspread, and I fucked her. Hard, fast, pounding into the mattress. Then I flipped over to my back and watched her ride.

My wife was beautiful when she rode me.

I palmed her breasts again, loving the way her nipples pebbled against my palms. She rocked her hips before putting her hands on my chest and sliding up and down my length. Needing more, knowing she did too, I gripped her hips, kept her steady, then fucked her from below. It was hard and fast and messy and everything I loved.

When she came again, I followed her, because I didn't need anything else, I just needed her.

She collapsed on top of me, and I held her close, running my hand up and down her back.

"We need to hurry."

"I know. We don't have much time."

We quickly rinsed off, cleaning up the mess and making the bed as fast as we could. We didn't even bother touching each other in the shower. Because I knew if we did, we'd get distracted, and then we'd be late.

As soon as we opened the door, and I made sure that Devney's sex hair wasn't too sexed up, the front door opened and the sound of pounding feet hit our ears.

"Mom! Silver met a boy!"

I sighed. The twins were growing up far too fast.

"I did not. I just talked to a boy from school. I didn't meet him."

"Yes, you did!"

"No, I didn't!"

Devney gave me a look, grinned, and we walked out to the living room to see our twins, blond-haired and blue-eyed, just like their mom, fighting.

They were fraternal twins, not quite identical, but they had the same look about them.

And, as always, they were fighting.

Kennedy was more outgoing, Silver a little more introverted, but they were best friends, and loved to fight. It was their love language.

Considering me and my brothers, and Devney and her horde of a family, it made sense.

"Stop fighting, girls. Tell me how your day was."

"Oh, we have stories," Addison said as she came in, Paisley right behind her. The women set down shopping bags and threw themselves on the couch.

"Seriously, it was a day."

"I'm just glad that you guys had mall duty, and I didn't."

"Like we would let you go with us to the mall, Dad," Kennedy said with a fake sneer, and I narrowed my gaze at her.

"Tone."

"Sorry!" Silver apologized for them both for some reason, and I sighed.

I watched both Paisley and Addison laugh with the

girls, and I was grateful for their girl trip. Devney had to work that morning, a conference call she couldn't get out of, even though her boss probably would've taken it for her. But it was good for us to have some alone time, even if we'd had to have a quickie in the middle of our day.

Greer walked in behind them, finally closing the door.

"Sorry, phone. Anyway, the twins were great. Promise."

"They were," Paisley agreed.

"If you say so."

"Dad," both girls whined, before they tried to tackle me. I fell back onto the ground playfully, since we had perfected this move over the past twelve years.

The fact that my baby girls would be teenagers in less than two months still worried me.

How the hell had that happened?

But it didn't matter. Because this was my family.

We had changed and grown over the years, had broken and found peace.

I smiled at my wife as she talked to her friends, her family, and let the girls beat me up.

I had come to Denver to find family. To make one.

It turns out I already had one all along, and now it was growing.

My girls had the love of my life's eyes.

And her smile.

What more did I need?

A Note from Carrie Ann Ryan

Thank you so much for reading **GOOD TIME BOYFRIEND**.

Oops! I wrote a rom-com! I didn't mean to, even with the emotional drama of these characters, but I LOVED writing them. And I'm so happy with how these characters are changing the game.

Next time? You get to see Luca's past....

And Addison's future.

And if you'd like to read about Greer's story with her two men, you can read it in Best Friend Temptation!

The First Time Series:
Book 1: Good Time Boyfriend
Book 2: Last Minute Fiancé
Book 3: Second Chance Husband

NEXT IN THE FIRST TIME SERIES:
Addison and Luca are ready….they think.
Maybe. Last Minute Fiancé.

IF YOU'D LIKE TO READ A BONUS SCENE:
CHECK OUT THIS SPECIAL EPILOGUE!

If you want to make sure you know what's coming next from me, you can sign up for my newsletter at www. CarrieAnnRyan.com; follow me on twitter at @CarrieAnnRyan, or like my Facebook page. I also have a Facebook Fan Club where we have trivia, chats, and other goodies. You guys are the reason I get to do what I do and I thank you.

Make sure you're signed up for my MAILING LIST so you can know when the next releases are available as well as find giveaways and FREE READS.

Happy Reading!

Also from Carrie Ann Ryan

The Montgomery Ink Legacy Series:

Book 1: Bittersweet Promises

Book 2: At First Meet

Book 2.5: Happily Ever Never

Book 3: Longtime Crush

Book 4: Best Friend Temptation

Book 4.5: Happily Ever Maybe

Book 5: Last First Kiss

Book 6: His Second Chance

Book 7: One Night with You

The Wilder Brothers Series:

Book 1: One Way Back to Me

Book 2: Always the One for Me

Book 3: The Path to You
Book 4: Coming Home for Us
Book 5: Stay Here With Me
Book 6: Finding the Road to Us
Book 7: Moments for You
Book 8: A Wilder Wedding
Book 9: Forever For Us

The First Time Series:
Book 1: Good Time Boyfriend
Book 2: Last Minute Fiancé
Book 3: Second Chance Husband

The Aspen Pack Series:
Book 1: Etched in Honor
Book 2: Hunted in Darkness
Book 3: Mated in Chaos
Book 4: Harbored in Silence
Book 5: Marked in Flames

The Montgomery Ink: Fort Collins Series:
Book 1: Inked Persuasion
Book 2: Inked Obsession
Book 3: Inked Devotion
Book 3.5: Nothing But Ink
Book 4: Inked Craving

Book 5: Inked Temptation

The Montgomery Ink: Boulder Series:
Book 1: Wrapped in Ink
Book 2: Sated in Ink
Book 3: Embraced in Ink
Book 3: Moments in Ink
Book 4: Seduced in Ink
Book 4.5: Captured in Ink
Book 4.7: Inked Fantasy
Book 4.8: A Very Montgomery Christmas

Montgomery Ink: Colorado Springs
Book 1: Fallen Ink
Book 2: Restless Ink
Book 2.5: Ashes to Ink
Book 3: Jagged Ink
Book 3.5: Ink by Numbers

Montgomery Ink Denver:
Book 0.5: Ink Inspired
Book 0.6: Ink Reunited
Book 1: Delicate Ink
Book 1.5: Forever Ink
Book 2: Tempting Boundaries
Book 3: Harder than Words

Also from Carrie Ann Ryan

Book 3: Far From Destined
Book 4: From Our First

The Less Than Series:
Book 1: Breathless With Her
Book 2: Reckless With You
Book 3: Shameless With Him

The Fractured Connections Series:
Book 1: Breaking Without You
Book 2: Shouldn't Have You
Book 3: Falling With You
Book 4: Taken With You

The Whiskey and Lies Series:
Book 1: Whiskey Secrets
Book 2: Whiskey Reveals
Book 3: Whiskey Undone

The Gallagher Brothers Series:
Book 1: Love Restored
Book 2: Passion Restored
Book 3: Hope Restored

The Ravenwood Coven Series:
Book 1: Dawn Unearthed

Also from Carrie Ann Ryan

Book 2: Dusk Unveiled
Book 3: Evernight Unleashed

The Talon Pack:
Book 1: <u>Tattered Loyalties</u>
Book 2: <u>An Alpha's Choice</u>
Book 3: <u>Mated in Mist</u>
Book 4: <u>Wolf Betrayed</u>
Book 5: <u>Fractured Silence</u>
Book 6: <u>Destiny Disgraced</u>
Book 7: <u>Eternal Mourning</u>
Book 8: <u>Strength Enduring</u>
Book 9: <u>Forever Broken</u>
Book 10: Mated in Darkness
Book 11: Fated in Winter

Redwood Pack Series:
Book 1: <u>An Alpha's Path</u>
Book 2: <u>A Taste for a Mate</u>
Book 3: <u>Trinity Bound</u>
Book 3.5: <u>A Night Away</u>
Book 4: <u>Enforcer's Redemption</u>
Book 4.5: <u>Blurred Expectations</u>
Book 4.7: <u>Forgiveness</u>
Book 5: <u>Shattered Emotions</u>
Book 6: <u>Hidden Destiny</u>
Book 6.5: <u>A Beta's Haven</u>

Book 7: <u>Fighting Fate</u>

Book 7.5: <u>Loving the Omega</u>

Book 7.7: <u>The Hunted Heart</u>

Book 8: <u>Wicked Wolf</u>

The Elements of Five Series:

Book 1: From Breath and Ruin

Book 2: From Flame and Ash

Book 3: From Spirit and Binding

Book 4: From Shadow and Silence

Dante's Circle Series:

Book 1: <u>Dust of My Wings</u>

Book 2: <u>Her Warriors' Three Wishes</u>

Book 3: <u>An Unlucky Moon</u>

Book 3.5: <u>His Choice</u>

Book 4: <u>Tangled Innocence</u>

Book 5: <u>Fierce Enchantment</u>

Book 6: <u>An Immortal's Song</u>

Book 7: <u>Prowled Darkness</u>

Book 8: Dante's Circle Reborn

Holiday, Montana Series:

Book 1: <u>Charmed Spirits</u>

Book 2: <u>Santa's Executive</u>

Book 3: <u>Finding Abigail</u>

Book 4: <u>Her Lucky Love</u>

Also from Carrie Ann Ryan

Book 5: Dreams of Ivory

The Branded Pack Series:
(Written with Alexandra Ivy)
Book 1: <u>Stolen and Forgiven</u>
Book 2: <u>Abandoned and Unseen</u>
Book 3: <u>Buried and Shadowed</u>

About the Author

Carrie Ann Ryan is the New York Times and USA Today
bestselling author of contemporary, paranormal, and
young adult romance. Her works include the Montgomery Ink, Redwood Pack, Fractured Connections, and
Elements of Five series, which have sold over 3.0 million
books worldwide. She started writing while in graduate
school for her advanced degree in chemistry and hasn't

stopped since. Carrie Ann has written over seventy-five novels and novellas with more in the works. When she's not losing herself in her emotional and action-packed worlds, she's reading as much as she can while wrangling her clowder of cats who have more followers than she does.

www.CarrieAnnRyan.com